BOBERT AND THE WARLORD

This is a work of satirical fiction. Names, faces, and places are more or less a product of the author's fairly limited imagination, and therefore are more or less fairly fictitious and absolutely not directly inspired by real-life events. Any resemblance to actual persons, particularly dead ones, events, particularly dumb ones, or locales, particularly notable ones, are entirely due to the author's complete lack of creativity. If not for the First Amendment of the United States Constitution, I would be clean out of work. Any copyright infringement was entirely unintentional, and a further outgrowth of the author's lack of skill.

Copyright © 2021 by Kerless Hopps

Cover art by Melissa Neel

ISBN 979-8-7831-7579-4 (paperback)

AS TRANSLATED BY KERLESS HOPPS

For Kelly, the best friend a man could ever hope to have.

For Rocket, the first honest-to-God fan I ever had.

And for all the women who claimed I would never make it.
They're still laughing.

BOBERT AND THE WARLORD

A recap of Part the First, or, Bobert and the Silversmith

In Part the First, Bobert the Frog, democratically elected folk hero of Croak, was pulled from his bed by a hysterical farmer. The farmer brought Bobert to his farm, and Bobert learned that a snail thief was on the loose. Not just any snail thief however, for there was a mystery surrounding this one. It was impossibly strong, and it seemed entirely unperturbed by what at all rights ought to have been a crippling wound.

Bobert's efforts to track the thief came to naught, and he decided to follow another lead; the thief's leg was terribly damaged. To follow this lead, he turned to a good friend of his, Amphibia the innkeeper, who put him on the right track. Bobert spoke with the widow of a silversmith whose leg had been damaged before he died, in much the same way as the farmer had described, though this too seemed to come to naught. In a last-ditch effort to make some headway on the case, Bobert decided to follow the thief, if he returned to the farm for another snail that night. It was a high hope, but Bobert was desperate.

So the night found Bobert following a limping Frog deep into the dangerous forest. At last Bobert came to a clearing which held the ruins of an ancient pagan altar surrounded by four mysterious arches. Bobert followed the trail through the northernmost arch, and entered a deep cave system which brought him to a cavernous, well, cavern[1]. Here he found cages full of zombies, and after his initial meeting with the mysterious and powerful Necromancer, Bobert fought and killed them all[2]. At last he was faced only with a snake, but in killing it, he transmuted it into a Beast many times worse. Bobert was nearly killed by the Beast, but luckily Amphibia showed up at the last moment, and with a few well-placed arrows she saved the day, forcing the Beast to flee.

Bobert and Amphibia then turned to a local scholar, Grogory, to confirm Bobert's suspicions, and Grogory told them how to defeat the Necromancer. So Bobert and Amphibia went once more to the caves, where they confronted the Necromancer at his dinner, and while he was laughing maniacally, Arnold the Silversmith, a hyper-intelligent zombie who retained the memories of his past life for mysterious reasons, conked him on the head. Bobert finished the Necromancer off, Amphibia saved Arnold's unlife, and the town, with the addition of one zombie silversmith, went on as though the past two days had never happened. After all, such adventures were commonplace in the town of Croak.

---

[1] Though there may be many synonyms for both cavernous (vast, expansive, capacious, sepulchral), and cavern (cave, grotto, chamber), the only other acceptable pairing in this context would be 'sepulchral grotto', and that is solely for the epic implications of such a phrasing.
[2] So much for Zombie Rights. What do we want? Brains! When do we want them? Brains!

BOBERT AND THE WARLORD

Bobert and the Shade
Part the Second, or, Bobert and the Warlord

Four long months had passed since Bobert and Amphibia had destroyed the Necromancer, and seen his caves sealed off. The first month had passed rather quietly, with relatively few attacks of any kind around Croak. There had been some resistance to Arnold's presence, but after the parents had all determined that he had no desire to devour the brains of their children, most of the town had accepted him. There had been one incident where a large group of young men had come to Bobert in quite bad shape, but after an hour or so of interrogation which may or may not have involved a bright light and a few white lies, it turned out that they had attacked Arnold, not vice versa, and had learned just why necromancers like zombies. The violence against Arnold, at least, had stopped soon after that.

The second month, however, had not gone quite as smoothly as the first. Bobert had been kept on his toes by a sudden influx of violent and dangerous creatures into the area. He had spent nearly every day fighting something or another; a mouse clan migrating south looking to carve territory out of a warmer land on Tuesday, nomadic squirrel mounted Frogan raiders still clinging to the old ways on Wednesday, and armed Lizard warriors every other day of the week. Bobert had even had to do battle with a pack of were-frogs that had sought to make prey of the Croakan residents, and for nearly two weeks the town had been terrorized by a dark and terrifying bat before Bobert had tracked it to its sepulchrous lair on the outskirts of town, to slay it while it was yet to bright for the devilish beast to escape.

He had been joined in the defense of Croak by Tad, a veteran soldier of Croak's militia, which had long since been disbanded from disuse[3], and a green Forest Ranger, Cat Frills, who had become an official Forest Ranger just days before, and had been sent to the area. They had lightened the load tremendously, and Bobert had been freed to look into just why so many threats had come to Croak at once. They were not fleeing some evil in the north, for they came from every direction, nor were there rumors of wealth in Croak to lead them there, as was often the case. No, these beasts seemed drawn to Croak by something even they did not fully recognize or understand. Many of them didn't even know that they had been drawn there. But that much was clear to Bobert: something was bringing worse and worse creatures to Croak, and his investigation was better aimed at discovering what.

He had not made much progress on that front, however, before the third month had come, and brought with it such an influx of enemies that even with the help of Tad and Cat, Bobert had struggled to protect the town. So, on the advice of Amphibia and Tad, Bobert had swallowed his pride and called for a town meeting. He had asked for volunteers to protect the town, and two had responded. A young nobleman, a noble-

---

[3] Croak's militia had been disbanded about two months after Bobert, still a young man, had been democratically elected the town's folk hero. Mostly the townspeople simply didn't want to pay to arm a group of people to do what one apparently could do.

boy, in Bobert's mind, had approached the stand, and behind him had trailed the largest brute that Bobert had ever seen, who by the looks of him had more than a drop of Bullfrog in him. The boy had introduced himself as Dante, a young nobleman's son on a journey of self-discovery[4], and his enormous companion he introduced as Bjorn Giant, a lovable-yet-dangerous, well-meaning, part-Bullfrog toad. He had announced to the town that the call to adventure had brought them to Croak, to investigate rumors of strange happenings, and as such he, and consequently his friend Bjorn, had agreed to join Bobert's squad, and had remained over the last few weeks, being surprisingly helpful for a near-child and a gentle giant.

About a week after the meeting another joined the squad, a knight of the Order of the Light One. Sir Beren, as he had introduced himself, had asked to join Bobert, to further the mission given him by the monk of his monastery to investigate this same sudden increase in attacks. Sir Beren too had proven a useful ally, an intelligent man and accomplished warrior, so good as to nearly match Bobert in skill, though he was yet hot-headed at times.

Despite the size and determination of his squad, which now counted six and was incredibly fierce, Bobert had barely had time to investigate the migration of monsters through Croak, for he was constantly leading his squad to defend the town and surrounding neighborhoods from marauding gangs of raiders. In particular, he had been having trouble with an influx of Lizards, barbarians from the south mingling with tribal warriors of the forest to create roving warbands with a great hatred for all Frogs.

It was just such a warband that Bobert and his trusty allies were battling now, in a small neighborhood of toads, one of the terrestrial neighborhoods which made up the ground layer of Croak. He was in a small courtyard, and several portable merchant's stalls lined the street, broken and empty; their goods, now scattered across the square, had been looted by the raiders which now lay dead, slain at the hands of Bobert's protection squad. Several of the stalls were on fire, their flames creating a hot ring which trapped the two sides in a small, violent circle. Bobert's men were scattered around the courtyard, each fighting his own

---

4 By which Bobert had known he was true; only the entitled feel the need for so-called 'self-discovery'. Everyone else is more worried about discovering food and money.

battle against unfair odds; holding their own, but much too preoccupied to help their leader. Bobert stood with his back against the fountain, warding his enemies away with a wickedly sharp axe.

His enemies were seven Lizards, all closing in with the grim determination to take him out of the battle even if it cost them their lives, so that they would have fame at least in death, as was the way in the pseudo-cult that was their religion. Three of them had forsaken their weapons and were licking their sharp teeth with bifurcated tongues, waiting for the right moment to pounce and rip into Bobert's flesh. The other four were equipped with crude swords better for slaughtering than fighting, and leather shields with backs of bronze; weapons, Bobert knew, of southern origin, which told him he was dealing with marauders infamous for their brutality.

They had him flanked, and looked as though they knew it, but they did not take their apparent advantage too much for granted. The warlike Lizards were accustomed to soft, peaceful, often cowardly Frogs, but when they saw one charging in to face them with an axe held high in one hand, and a smooth iron shield in the other, leading five others with mismatching armor and weapons, they knew that they were facing Bobert the Protector and his loyal soldiers, and they knew that though they faced Frogs, they faced Frogs hardened by battle, ferocious as snakes and bloodthirsty as cats. Yet even knowing this, it seems they had been surprised to find just how well the Frogs fought, for Bobert was not in the habit of leaving his enemies alive long enough to report his numbers or ferocity back to his enemies, to help him retain the element of surprise. So as these seven Lizards approached the Frog with the axe and shield, they approached cautiously. Not that it did them much good. One took a swing, and lost his arm. One tried to edge him away from the battle, and had his shield split by a flurry of blows, and his head soon parted from his body. Another took advantage of Bobert's turned back and leapt at him with an upraised weapon, but was slammed to the ground with an axe in his gut. A Lizard grasped Bobert's now empty hand with his tongue, but Bobert pulled him in and smashed in the Lizard's face with his shield edge. Within moments all seven Lizards lay dead around him. He pulled his axe out of the corpse of the last one, and looked around the square to see if his companions needed any help.

BOBERT AND THE WARLORD

Bjorn Giant was looming over five Lizards, his mace hanging forgotten in his right hand as he swung a sixth Lizard by its tail in his left, beating the Lizards that surrounded him with their companion. Despite being a gentle giant to his friends, Bjorn was a force to be reckoned with, when you violated his moral code[5].

Dante was faced by three Lizards. He had a delighted smile on his face, his rapier in his right hand, and his cape was draped over his left arm. As one of the Lizards leapt forward, Bobert saw Dante strike like a snake, using the cloak to bat his opponent's blade away, and before the Lizard could react his throat had been cut open. Bobert had once tried Dante's cape and sword, but had somehow gotten his leg tangled in the cape, and would have impaled himself on the sword had Bjorn not sympathetically lifted him bodily from the ground.

Tad was fighting back to back with Sir Beren, for the two of them had become friends in their time fighting together. Tad was using his round shield for offense as much as his longsword, while Sir Beren fought with a warhammer nearly as tall as he was, wearing a suit of plate mail that reflected the fires in the courtyard to give him the look of a vengeful spirit of light. His enemies shrank back from him, but nonetheless his hammer flashed through the air, and smashed into them with audible crunches that collapsed them to the ground or sent them reeling backwards.

Cat Frills was kneeling on a log with his bow, his arrows stuck in the ground beside him. He was shooting any Lizard that he saw, and he didn't miss a single shot. The last kill went to Cat, for everyone else had slain their opponents, and the last Lizard was fleeing, when Cat shot it through the back of the neck, causing it to fall limply forward.

"The key to a good shot," Cat told no one in general, "Is to make sure your shoulders are pleasantly relaxed."

With their enemies felled, the heroes leapt into action, forming a bucket line to put out the fires that the raiding Lizards had started. A fountain stood in the very center of the square, which depicted a tall,

---

[5] Bjorn had a somewhat simplistic moral code, the sort taught to children who are not yet old enough to understand context. For Bjorn, being nice was good and being mean was bad, and this was enough. His enormity and stringent, albeit simplistic, morality were enough to make it obvious to him that his only calling in life, as he had once told Dante, was to make bullies be nice.

graceful, scantily clad young tree Frog showing off everything and then some to the houses[6] around the street, carved from a fine marble mined from the caves beneath Croak.

It was from this fountain that they drew water, handing the buckets to Bjorn, whose great height allowed him to more easily put out the fires, and when they had done what they could, the group collapsed exhaustedly around the fountain, bandaging their wounds and catching their breath in silence. It was Dante who spoke first, his thick, gentry accent cutting through the air as Bjorn carefully handed him a towel.

"Grazie," the noble-boy thanked Bjorn in his native tongue. "This fight has, how to say? exhausted me. But mayhap we shall all sleep soon enough, eh?"

The older veteran, Tad, gave Dante a chilling stare as he answered. "I've seen more wars than you've lived years, boy. I'll not be killed by a bunch of slimy Lizards."

"Be nice, Tad Toad," the half-Bullfrog Bjorn rumbled (he had a peculiar habit of always adding a descriptor to people's names). "Or Bjorn Giant will have to make you hug. Mamma always made Bjorn Giant hug when he was not nice."

The forest ranger, Cat, gave a loud laugh. "Surely your mother couldn't make you do anything, Giant! It seems to me that men with your strength and stature are truly free as the wind and fierce as the lion!"

Bjorn looked at Cat with wide eyes, and in a conspiratorial whisper, as though his mother was just over his shoulder, said, "But Momma is scary!"

Sir Beren nodded wisely, not looking up from the armor he was cleaning, which bore the insignia of his holy order. "We all have our fears, Cat. Dante fears the hustle and bustle of court. Tad fears the relaxation of retirement. These are wise fears. Court is deadlier than any sword, and rest steals the soul until the body is a husk. Bjorn fears a mother. I dare say that Bjorn is the wisest among us."

---

[6] The houses in this courtyard were favored, for some unfathomable reason, by the older merchants whose work kept them away from home too often to start a family.

BOBERT AND THE WARLORD

"Cat Frills fears nothing!" The ranger boasted.

Sir Beren looked up at Cat with a twinkle in his eyes. "Then Cat Frills is a fool."

"Cat Frills is no fool!" He leapt to his feet, and struck a pose for each simile. "Cat Frills is as strong as a Bullfrog! As fast as a rabbit! As agile as a cat! As cunning as a snake!"

"Speed and strength, agility and cunning, these things are not wisdom, Master Cat." Dante put in, looking amused.

"The boy is right," Tad said.

"Wisdom is found not in the body, but in the mind." Sir Beren said mildly.

"What do you know, Sir Beren? Sitting around and reading dusty tomes in dusty rooms? Cat Frills will have none of that. Cat Frills would rather scale a mountain, or ford a wild river!"

Sir Beren simply laughed with Dante and Tad, while Cat looked furious that no one would take him seriously. Bjorn, on the other hand, looked confused, and slightly suspicious. "Does Bjorn Giant need to make all of you hug?"

Bobert finally spoke. "No, Bjorn, that is quite all right. Cat, stop boasting, none here care. I dare say that all of us here have done more notable things in our lives than you, with the sole exception perhaps of Dante, due to youth. Dante, Sir Beren, stop egging him on. Save such amusement for less precious times. Tad, come with me, let us search for survivors. The rest of you, try to clean up this courtyard. Keep an eye on the fires, stand up the stalls and clear all the rubble. Make a large pyre with the bad wood. We shall burn these Lizards; it will be cleaner than piling them up and quicker than burying them."

The night found Bobert's Heroes, as the People[7] called them, at Amphibia's Inn for a victory brew. They were greeted by applause when

---

[7] There are two types of 'people'. There are people, by which I mean the generic term for people you don't know and don't really care about, whose opinion is completely irrelevant to the sane and practical person's life.

And then there are the People, that great, terrifying, faceless entity. The People were the jeering crowd as the Salem Witches burned. The People were the awful, silent masses at the beheading of Louis XVI. The People are the armies on either side of a battlefield, and the People are the they entered, and had happily accepted the free drinks, claiming a table together and ordering a small feast which they paid for with the loot taken off the raiders. Bobert, however, did not join them, instead taking a seat at the end of the bar, far away from his men. While they laughed and drank and patted each other on the back, he sat in brooding silence, once more contemplating the problem which had now plagued his thoughts for two months: Where were these raiders coming from, and where, or to whom, were they going? Bobert hardly noticed the cheer that announced the arrival of his squad's dinner, and when a plate of steaming[8] stew was pushed under his nose, he looked up to find Amphibia standing there with a small bowl of candied ants in her other hand.

"I didn't pay for this," Bobert said.

"You don't pay here," she said. "You know that."

"You haven't eaten yet. Care to join me?" Bobert asked as Amphibia placed the candied ants beside the stew.

"Don't mind if I do," she answered, striding off as she untied her apron, and returning a few moments later with a second bowl of stew and two mucky glasses.

"It seems candles are in order," Bobert noted dryly, nodding to the glasses.

Amphibia huffed as she pulled up a stool and sat across the bar from him. "I would take Lizards over customers without hesitation some days. And you look as though you've had an equally long day. Are the recruits wearing on your nerves?"

"No," Bobert answered. "Well, yes. But that isn't what's on my mind."

---

mobs in the street. The opinion of the People matters immensely, for the People are a great, vengeful, man-made deity with a penchant for mass-murder.

[8] The Sapient Frog, that is, the Anura Sapiens, like most sapient species developed the use of fire early on, and their digestive systems developed to make use of the new tool. Modern Anura Sapiens are rather fond of hot food, as it helps their bodies to absorb the heat they need to stay awake.

BOBERT AND THE WARLORD

"Tell me," Amphibia said, half-prompting and half-ordering him.

"These raids," Bobert said. "They aren't normal. They are too frequent, and some of these Lizards are properly trained."

"Trained? But Lizards in this region are still tribal barbarians," Amphibia protested. "They receive no training. They simply have weapons put in their hands and are sent on raids."

"Not these," Bobert told her. "They were no great warriors, but they were trained in war nonetheless. And they carried bronze weapons. These were southern Lizards."

"What were they doing here, then? It would take them months to travel here!"

"That is what worries me," Bobert answered. Before he could continue his thought, however, a commotion outside caused him to turn in time to see the door to the inn fly open.

A Praying Mantis, clothed in muddy robes, stumbled out of the dark, exhausted and half-starved. He seemed to have walked for several hours, and was, as far as Bobert could tell, in shock, no doubt from whatever had caused his robes to be filthy and blood-soaked. Sir Beren, upon seeing the newcomer, leapt to his feet, and rushed to the side of the Mantis.

"Brother!" He cried, in great distress at the state of the monk. "What has happened to you? Who would dare assault a servant of the Light One?!"

The Mantis grasped Sir Beren upon the shoulder, his voice shaking and exhausted, half-delirious. "Sir Beren. Thank the Light One. I need help. I seek the hero. The Light One spoke to me, and told me to find him, a Frog named Bobert. Do you know of him? Can you help me find him?"

Hearing the monk's words, Bobert strode forward to stand before the Mantis.

"The nearest monastery, as far as I can remember, lies many miles to the south. What brings you to Croak, Brother?" Bobert asked.

"You are Bobert?"

"I am," Bobert replied, "Though I was not aware that the monasteries cared for me one way or another."

"We care for all peoples, hero, but that is not why I have come. I have been commanded to seek your help. My monastery has been attacked, and I fear the worst. T'was a cruel enemy that brought war to our place of peace, and slaughtered my Brothers."

"Come, sit next to the fire," Sir Beren encouraged the Mantis, as he closed the door and led the Mantis through the room to the crackling hearth. Amphibia materialized a moment later with a steaming mug that the Mantis gratefully took and gulped from, shivering as the warmth coursed through his body.

"Spare no detail," Bobert commanded, and his squad, joined by Amphibia and what patrons remained in the inn, fell silent to hear the monk's words.

"It began a night ago," the Mantis began quietly. "My brethren and I live in a monastery, a temple dedicated to the Light One, holy is his name. We were performing our rituals, asking for the rising of the sun, as we do every night, and we were nearing completion.

"As we prayed, however, a great howling went up outside the doors, as though the wind had been called forth by the Dark One to destroy our humble monastery. The wind howled through the trees and beat against the doors, and it slipped through cracks in our windows and brought a smell of smoke and death, a terrible stench to the cathedral where we prayed. My brothers and I grew afraid of the wind, so naturally we all bowed our heads to the Light One, begging that He remove the stench, and becalm the wind. In his great wisdom, however, our Light One did not see fit to lend us His strength, and He withheld from us His warmth, nor did he lift the fear from our heart's, for he wished, I suppose, to test our faith.

"As we prayed, the candles upon the altar burned out, our Light One's way to spare my life, that I might continue to serve Him, and I volunteered to go to the cupboards in the kitchen, and fetch some new ones. Being holy candles as they were, to be placed upon the altar itself, they had to be treated in holy water, to remove the impurities from them, the essence of sin which their maker imbued them with. So I went to the kitchen, and was there, consecrating the candles with sacred rites and holy water, when I heard from behind me the doors to the cathedral slam open with a horrendous screech. I knew it was them, for they are the only doors which squeak, since I oiled the hinges of the others, but was called to prayer before I could oil them. I poked my head around the corner to investigate who came through the door, thinking perhaps a brother had returned from a mission trip in need of assistance, when I saw it, and hid myself."

A hush fell on the crowd so quiet that Bobert could have heard a pin drop, and the Mantis continued so quietly that the crackling of the fire blended with his words.

"I saw a Lizard, great and tall, with horned skin and sharp scales. He wore great metal plates of armor, so large a Frog could not lift them, and he carried a huge mace with bloodied spikes. His helm was wrought in a terrifying manner, like a melding between a snake and a dragon, with many ridges of horns, and two great fangs between which he looked, with eyes as red as anger.

"The Lizard stood in the doorway as his lessers poured into the hall, a despicable assortment of marauders and barbarians. The Lizard horde began to slaughter my brethren, and we were defenseless, being in a house of peace, and forbidden to acts of violence. As the Lizards slaughtered they fed, using their teeth to kill as much as their weapons. The large one joined, and with every swing he was as likely to kill his own as one of my Brothers, but the death of his minions seemed only to amuse him.

"The Lizards feasted that night, on my Brothers, on our provisions, even on their own dead. Eventually they all fell into a stupor, the snake-helmed one sitting at the top of the hall upon the altar like a throne. When I was sure they were asleep, I snuck out of my hiding place, and throughout the hall trying to see if one of my Brethren had survived, but none had. They must have imprisoned my fellow Faithful somewhere, for there were not enough bodies to count for all of us. Finally, I gave up my search in despair, and fled the hall. I walked for a while, until I grew too weary to continue, and when I could stumble no further I found a comfortable place to rest, and I fell into a dreamless sleep.

"Dreamless, that is, until I received a vision from the Light One. I saw the great sun shining brightly onto a corpse-filled valley, and on a cliff overlooking this valley I saw the Hero of Justice, with his blazing sword whiter than snow held high. I saw a great shadow on the land, which blocked the sun from view, a dark and dreadful cloud of black smoke, and from this cloud there burst a terrible beast unlike any I had ever seen, snake-like yet not, winged and vicious. The beast did battle with the Hero of Justice, and as it approached I saw a rider upon its back, though his face was hidden in shadow. The valley, beast, and Hero all dissipated, and the scene changed to this very inn. A man sat at the bar, and he looked over to me, saying, 'Find the hero Bobert in the village of Croak, in the inn of Amphibia."

The Mantis' tale hung heavy on the air when he finished speaking. Bobert sat with his head hung down, but when he raised his head, his eyes shone with a fierce, furious fire.

"I'll find him," he swore, "and he shall feel my fury."

But at what cost, Bobert did not yet know.

Dark grey clouds threatened rain on the squat stone monastery when Bobert's Heroes first saw the confused mass of tangled hallways and tiny courtyards sticking out of the forest like an ugly pimple. The windows were dark, and the heavy wooden doors were closed, so that at first sight the monastery would have seemed abandoned, but for the three Lizard guards that lounged around the main entrance, which led into the chapel. Bobert and his men approached the monastery through the twilight which seemed to creep across the land, and they paused in the treeline where the Lizards would yet be unable to see them.

The Lizard guards were short, skinny, and bright green, natives to the area, and clearly not as well-trained as many of their companions, for of the three guarding the door, two were asleep, and one was dozing in and out of consciousness. They were armed with chipped stone knives and axes, and small wooden shields, but their weapons laid abandoned around them, and their shields were used to protect them only from the elements.

With a silent signal to his companions, Bobert and Dante split off from the still group, sneaking around the edge of the treeline with all the stealth of the well-trained and light of foot, until the door and Lizard guards were hidden by the side of the building. They crossed stealthily to hide in the monastery's shadow, and began to sneak once more, this time back the way they came, to the corner of the building. Bobert peered around, and saw the three Lizard guards sleeping not twenty feet from where they stood.

BOBERT AND THE WARLORD

The dozing guard had now fallen as deeply asleep as his companions, and none of the three woke as Bobert and Dante snuck closer to them, each drawing a sharp and silent blade. They positioned themselves behind two of the Lizards, and with a nod from Bobert, clamped their hands over their victim's mouths and slit the Lizards' throats. The Lizards writhed and tried to cry out, but their calls for help were too muffled to even rouse their companion, and they died without any of their fellow raiders ever knowing of their demise. Dante dispatched the third in similar fashion as Bobert dragged their victims to the side and signaled for the rest of the Heroes, and they gathered around the entrance of the monastery without alerting any of the raiders that slept within.

The grates in the doors had been left open to allow the guards to easily communicate with the guarded, and they now allowed Bobert to peer into the monastery. A large group of Lizards were within, all in a drink-induced slumber. Several tables had been placed in a U shape, and they were covered in the remnants of a massive feast. The Lizards lay on the benches and tables, on the floor, and rolled against the wall. Many seemed to have simply passed out at some point, falling forward onto the table before them. But all of them slept with their weapons close by, and there were enough that the battle would be fierce. Bobert nodded to his men, and they all drew their weapons, readying themselves for the coming fight. He gave the monastery door a soft push, and it gave easily, swinging open. But he had forgotten the words of the monk, that those doors had hinges which were not oiled.

The doors uttered a horrible, horrendously loud screeching creak that echoed through the forest, causing Bobert and his Heroes to freeze on the spot as every one of the Lizards within woke with a jolt. As if on cue[9], the rain began to come down, a steady drizzle that quickly picked up to an outright downpour. The jolt of the rain pulled the Heroes out of their shock, and Bobert was the first through the doorway, followed quickly by Sir Beren, Tad, Cat, and Dante, with Bjorn pulling up the rear.

As Bobert neared the first of the Lizards, it was already too late; they had leapt to their feet, weapons in hand, and were prepared to

---

[9] Or perhaps on cue indeed. The weather on Bobert's world has a rather theatrical personality, and it is not uncommon for a hurricane to be interrupted by a sunny day for a young couple's first date.

fight. Bobert and his men went to work, spreading out to give themselves plenty of space to fight. Their enemies were fierce and quite upset, for their excessive drinking, and being rudely awoken by six rather loud Frogs, had led to killer hangovers. The Lizards met the Heroes with a dreadful crash, and fierce screams erupted from all around. They leapt at their enemies from tabletops, wielding bread knives, chairs, forks, and stale baguettes[10] as weapons.

Bobert had long ago learned to keep his eye on the battle, not the fight, so while all his companions were absorbed in defeating the enemies in front of them, only he saw the enemies at the back of the hall, a group of Lizards twenty-strong that were heaving upon a great set of double doors. As the doors cracked open, a huge hand stuck out and grasped the edge of one, a hand the size of Bobert's torso. The Lizards, seeing this hand, backed quickly away from the double doors, and crossed the hall swiftly to push their way through a second door, disappearing down a dark hallway as the giant hand pushed the great doors open, and a huge, muscular arm came into view.

A huge Bullfrog, twice the size of Bjorn with ease, pushed the doors open with its shoulders as it lumbered through into the chapel where they fought. This Frog was alarmingly large, with a huge, round body to juxtapose its muscular arms. Two huge chins swung like pendulums beneath one foul face, and two large eyes stared around the room dumbly. The Bullfrog focused on Bobert and his men and lurched towards them, each step shaking the chapel with the force of an earthquake.

As the remaining Lizards scattered away from the lumbering giant, Bobert's men began to look around for the source of their fear. All eyes focused on the Bullfrog, and it broke into an all out charge, aiming for Bjorn, who stood before the doors to the forest outside and settled into a wrestling stance. The two met like a clash of thunder, the large giant and the small, and the Bullfrog was thrown by means of his own momentum through the doors of the chapel. As Bjorn and the Bullfrog

---

[10] The last of which were by far the most dangerous. It is a little known fact, but the French once fought an entire civil war with stale baguettes. Neither side won, but both suffered.

disappeared into the night, Bobert and the rest of his Heroes abandoned pursuit of the Lizards, and instead rushed outside to slay the giant Frog.

The giant was struggling to its feet in the mud, but before it could regain a good footing Bjorn had crashed into it once more, and the two collapsed into the mud in a heap of writhing, slippery flesh so tightly bound that Bobert and his Heroes could not hit the Bullfrog without fear of hurting Bjorn. Instead, they simply stood back, weapons at the ready to have at the giant if they found an opening.

The pair separated for a moment, and Bobert moved to attack, but Bjorn flung out an arm to stop him, and settled into a fighting stance. The giant grinned maliciously, and himself settled into a wide-bodied stance. They began to circle, and suddenly the fight began once more.

It was brute force against well-honed skill, for though the Bullfrog commanded enormous strength, Bjorn had spent years wrestling the biggest and baddest of the lands, and had learned much for when his strength was not enough. The Bullfrog caught Bjorn in his arms, and began to squeeze him with all his might, but Bjorn placed his hands upon the giant's head and pried upward until he was released. Bjorn in turn caught the giant's arm and tried to bend it straight at the elbow, but the giant merely flexed and Bjorn's grip was broken.

The two broke apart for a breath, and the giant broke the unspoken truce by throwing a punch at Bjorn, backed up by the force of a mountain. Bjorn skipped aside, and continuing the giant's present momentum, threw him against the monastery wall, cracking the heavy stone blocks. Bjorn beat at the dazed Bullfrog, but it was no good. With a single giant hand, and an audible grunt, the Bullfrog picked Bjorn up by the chest and slammed him into the ground. He raised both hands in a single fist to strike Bjorn, but before he could Bjorn had reared his legs above him and kicked him firmly in the grunt, causing the giant to stumble backwards.

With surprising agility for a Frog of his size, Bjorn leapt to his feet, but instead of continuing his attack on the once more charging Bullfrog, he reached over to the monastery wall, and dug his great fingers into one of the cracks that the Bullfrog had made. With rippling muscles and a roaring grunt, he pulled a great stone block out of the wall, and swung it around to crash it into the Bullfrog's head, stopping the giant dead in his tracks.

The Bullfrog went limp, collapsing lifelessly to the ground as a large wound on his head began to pour blood, and Bobert's Heroes looked at Bjorn the Giant with a newfound respect, all but Dante, who clasped Bjorn's forearm like a proud brother, beaming from ear to ear at Bjorn's great victory. After a brief round of congratulating the Giant on his victory, Bobert called his Heroes back to the task at hand.

"The remaining Lizards fled deeper into the monastery while we were preoccupied with the Bullfrog," Bobert told them. "Dante, Bjorn, go through the eastern portion of the monastery. Tad, Sir Beren, you take the west. Cat and I shall take the middle portion. Any who find the remaining Lizards, call if you find yourself in need of reinforcements."

Leaving the limp Bullfrog to bleed out in the rain, the squad dispersed once more into the monastery, each pair splitting off to explore one portion of the maze of hallways. It was dark and stormy night, and the monastery seemed to dance with shadows half-alive, but for every time Bobert spun with his sword poised to strike, lightning and shadow alone were found to be the culprit. Eventually he and Tad turned back, convinced that the Lizards were at the very least not in their portion of the monastery. When they made their way back to the entry chapel, they found the other four already returned, with similar reports; Tad and Sir Beren had found a few stragglers, but none would suffer themselves to be captured alive.

"But why such an interest in a mere monastery?" Dante asked, when Tad had finished their report on the western portion of the monastery. "We found nothing of much note, in our brief exploration."

"Nor we," Bobert replied, as Tad agreed. "I do not like this one bit. Even heathen Lizards do not lightly disrespect our holy places. I want you and Bjorn to investigate, and discover what secrets this place holds. Defend it if you can, should the Lizards return. Sir Beren, Tad, this was not the full force of the Lizards as described to us. They must have moved on, and left a smaller force to hold the monastery. Find their trail, and follow them. We must know where they are encamped. Cat and I shall follow those that fled from us tonight, and prevent them from returning to their masters. We will regroup here, or if the monastery is lost, in Croak."

BOBERT AND THE WARLORD

So, as Dante and Bjorn set to scouring every inch of the dreary monastery, and Sir Beren followed Tad southwards, Bobert found himself following an excitable and energetic Cat westwards. As they crested a small hill, Bobert looked back, and feared that he may have made a truly terrible mistake in breaking his Heroes up.

The trees above sheltered the forest floor from most of the rain, but the ground had nonetheless become slick and muddy. The Lizards were no doubt struggling with the wet conditions, being from drier climates, but Bobert and Cat had no difficulty making their way across the wet forest floor. Bobert predicted that they would be on the Lizards before the dawn of a new day, but Cat was far too focused on showcasing his tracking skills to listen to Bobert's assessment of the situation, so Bobert had no one to brag to when he turned out to be right.

The Lizards, some thirty of them in all, were sheltered at the base of a flat cliff which was doing little to nothing to protect them from the rain. They sat miserably huddled together, covered in scraps of fabric and thin blankets, unsuccessfully attempting to stay warm. For Bobert and Cat, the night was only mildly chilly, certainly not enough to cause them to slow, but the Lizards were from much further south and their bodies were not used to this cold, especially when exposed to the elements that were so foreign to their natural habitats; their cold-blooded, desert-acclimated bodies were aching for a sleep from which the Lizards would not return. While they huddled desperately to escape the cold, all they succeeded in doing was making themselves an easy mark for ambush.

The hill they were on ran up steeply from the forest floor, and towards the top the ground split into two distinct levels, one rising high above the other with flat cliff sides sloping upward from the ground until they reached a peak some fifty feet high, the other running on like normal. The tree line ran up with the hill and onto the peak, though it hung back from the cliffs some twenty feet.

Bobert and Cat stopped at the edge of the tree line nearest the Lizards and observed them for a moment. They came up with a plan[11] in

---

[11] Admittedly, their plan was one of those which would only work on the most unintelligent of enemies. Luckily, Lizards are renowned for their lack of intelligence, and are only considered sapient due to a typo in The Encyclopedic Guide to all Sapient and Non-Sapient Species, which won

hushed whispers, and then split up. Cat, remaining in the trees, darted away to the right as stealthily as he could manage. Bobert, however, began to collect branches and long reeds of grass. He kept a close eye on the top of the cliff, and thus saw when Cat arrived at the top with a large armful of stones. Cat dropped the stones, quickly searched the tree line for Bobert's signal, and, not having seen it, disappeared once more into the trees. Bobert turned back to his work, and found a large birch tree. He took out his knife and began to cut short strips of birch bark until he had a large pile. He collected his sticks, and with the adeptness that comes only to the most experienced of adventurers, he began to split one end of each stick, and to stuff it with birch bark. Soon he had some two dozen torches, which he tied to trees and low branches with the reeds. He retained only one torch, and went back to see if he could see Cat, whom he saw kneeling at the peak of the cliff looking down at the Lizards, surrounded by a pile of torches and a huge fire. Cat was looking deliberately away from the fire to preserve his night-vision, and saw Bobert, who waved his torch as a signal. Cat waved his own torch to confirm, and then turned, lighting all of his torches in his fire, stabbing their ends in the ground to keep the fire from being suffocated by the dirt. Bobert lit his torch with his tinderbox, and then went around, lighting all of the torches on the trees. Soon, the entire tree line seemed to be populated by torch-bearing Frogs, and the Lizards leapt to their feet in disarray, trying to untangle their weapons and armor while simultaneously not looking away from the phantom soldiers in the tree line. Bobert stuck his torch in the ground and ran to various places, stepping into the light just enough to reinforce the idea that there were more than a dozen Frogs present.

When the Lizards descended into chaos, Cat leapt into action, tossing brands among the enemies below, burning some and impaling others, for he had sharpened the ends of his torches, and made them longer than normal so he could throw them like spears. Several Lizards

---

the Most Uncreative Name For A Truly Boring Book three times in a row. A fourth Most Uncreative Name For A Truly Boring Book award was never awarded, as judges could not be found, due to the extremely high mortality rate from the judges dying of boredom.

fell to his attack before he threw his last spear. When he did, however, he did not stop. Instead, he went to the fire, and wrapping his hands in the thick leather of his armor, he began to throw the stones from the bottom of the fire into the midst of the Lizards, felling several even as they fled to the only opening that Bobert had seemingly left them, where he prepared to meet them in the shadows with sword drawn. Several of the Lizards leading the charge had grabbed up Cat's torches, and were awkwardly running with them, struggling to keep the ends from hitting the ground without tangling them in the branches overhead. Of the thirty odd Lizards that had been camped under the tent, only thirteen had managed to flee. As they approached, Bobert slipped into the shadows, and when the last passed he stepped out and struck him down, thus catching them from behind, making their brutal slaughter all the more brutal and, well, slaughterous. Once they were dead, and their torches extinguished, Bobert began the arduous work of dragging them all back to their makeshift camp. Cat was already down from the cliff, his fire completely extinguished, walking through the camp, dispatching any of the Lizards which had survived but were too injured to flee. Many of the Lizards did not have a scratch upon them, but were so burnt by the torches and hot rocks which carpeted the camp that they had collapsed from the pain, and either lay writhing or playing dead.

Bobert and Cat made a pile of the fallen Lizards, and piled the old brands and the burnables of their camp on them. They went into the tree line and collected the torches that Bobert had made and, wishing to spare the forest of a scene so morbid as a battlefield, they threw the torches still burning on the Lizards and watched as the cloth and wood caught flame. Bobert and Cat gathered fallen wood and limbs and threw these on as well, until the pile was large enough to burn through the night. Bobert settled down on the ground a ways away, upwind of the bonfire to avoid the smell of burning flesh, and pulled out his knife to whittle a piece of wood that he had stored in his ever-handy pack. He was just settling into a nice rhythm when Cat let out a violent and obviously fake cough.

"Yes?" Bobert asked patiently.

"Well, Bobert," Cat replied, "I was just curious why we're stopping here? We could make good progress back to the monastery before this adrenaline fades. In a survival situation, one should always make use of adrenaline if he can. It's an important natural resource. So come on! Let's get going!" As he spoke he began to hop from foot to foot, clapping his hands in an attempt to urge Bobert on.

Bobert adopted an obviously fake air of shocked confusion. "But Cat? Surely you know?"

Cat froze, balanced precariously on one foot, and cocked his head to one side like a curious child who has been shown a fascinating magic trick.

"Know what?" he asked, narrowing his eyes in suspicion.

Bobert laughed. "Why, I would have expected you of all people to know that you can never leave a fire unattended, especially in a forest. The sparks could fly, and light a leaf or piece of wood, causing a forest fire. Honestly, you should have known this, being a Forest Ranger, inexperienced though you are. I shall be taking the quality of your education up with Gramps. Even a bear knows that much."

Cat looked thoroughly confused at the mention of Gramps.

"Sorry," Bobert said. "Gramps is my contact at the Council of Forest Rangers. You probably know him by a different name. He never did like my calling him Gramps. Half of why the name stuck."

Cat laughed a little uncomfortably, "Yes, we probably knew him as something else. Professor Blah-Blah or something."

Bobert glanced at Cat. "The Council doesn't have Professors. They have Senior Rangers."

"I was joking," Cat said meekly.

"Ah."

The monastery was a menagerie of monastic motifs. Magnificent murals of magnanimous monks modestly mending the most malicious of maladies, complicated carvings of courageous conquerors combating the companies of corrupted cacodemons, pleasant paintings of paradisiacal places, perfected by the persistent pampering of their princely protectors, and splendid statues of the seraphic servants of the sacred Supreme, all decorated the many hallways and rooms of the monastery, many yet untouched by the raiding Lizards which had not made it much further than the entering chapel.

Hallways ran through the complex like a maze, and every few feet was an alcove containing a painting, a sculpture, a book, or something else, all in some way of a religious nature. Dante and Bjorn strolled through the monastery, now deep in its bowels, searching for some clue as to why a Lizard warlord would raid this place and leave its people to defend it. They spoke as they walked, debating what they would find.

"It contains a passage, sì, to Croak, in a dark forgotten cellar of the town hall. The Lizards wished to use this passage to quietly enter into Croak, sì? In the dark of night, as it were?"

Bjorn laughed at Dante's theory. "Why a tunnel, Dante Friend, and why to Croak? I think there is a weapon here, a big one that a Lizard would want. We'll find it, and Bobert Hero will give it to me, so that Lizard doesn't get it."

Dante looked incredulous. "Why would there be a weapon at a monastery, please? And why so big? No no, I think it more likely that there is a tunnel, don't you agree?"

"No. A tunnel is silly, Dante Friend. It is a weapon, that the monks keep to hide."

"To hide? Why would you hide a weapon in a monastery, amico? It is a-" suddenly he cocked his head to the side, like a predator alerted to the presence of prey.

"It is a what, Dante Friend?" said Bjorn, who was ahead and did not notice Dante's sudden alertness.

Dante motioned for his silence, and they stood listening. After a moment Dante stirred.

"I thought I'd heard something. A, what is the phrase, a bump in the night, no? L'uomo nero, as my people would say. The, uh, Bogeyman, I believe is said here? No doubt it was the wind, or a tree outside. Let us continue, Bjorn, and find this secret swiftly. I dislike this place."

As midnight grew near, many hours after they had set out, Tad and Sir Beren at last came to the end of the tracks they had been following.

Nestled snugly in a valley between many densely forested mountains, there was a camp the size of a small village, filled with tents. The camp had obviously been there for a few weeks, for it was well established. Trenches were dug around the entire circumference of the camp, with sharp wooden stakes lining the bottoms and the camp-side embankment. Wooden walls ten feet tall at their shortest stood after the trench, all of which had walkways at the top where defenders patrolled with torches and bows. Four bridges crossed the trench, one in each cardinal direction. Each bridge was protected by a thick gate, and Tad believed he could just make out by the light of a patroller's torch large barrels of oil above each gate, the sort used to repel besiegers. Torches along the walls made the trench and walls easy to make out in the darkness.

Within the walls, the numerous campfires lit up their surroundings well enough that Tad could largely make out the camp. In stark contrast to the order of the defenses, the tent city within was set up in a chaotic fashion. The only orderly bits were the four roads, which ran straight from the gates to the center of the camp, where there stood a large hall of fur and white, round wood for poles. The hall was well lit, even more so than the camp, and there appeared to be a feast within, which spilled out into the courtyard before it.

Tad could make out no more in the darkness, so he turned to Sir Beren, and suggested they make camp. Sir Beren agreed, looking terribly tired. They hiked to a ridge that Tad spotted, from which they would have a good view of the camp without being too obvious come morning. They went without a fire, for both agreed without speaking that a fire would be too obvious for a reconnaissance mission. They rolled out their bed sheets and Sir Beren found water, taking their bottles to refill, while Tad remained at the site and studied the movements of the patrols, looking for a weakness in their defenses. Sir Beren returned shortly, and Tad produced two cold biscuits and salty cured meat for them to eat in silence, and after this spartan supper Sir Beren settled down to sleep while Tad took up the first watch of the camp far below.

Tad was pleased that Bobert had paired him off with one who was content to work in silence. Tad was not a man of many words, and he did not find any comfort or pleasure in conversation. Nor did he trust anyone who did talk too much. In his experience, a man should say only what he needs to say, and no more. He did not approve of the Forest Ranger that Bobert had inducted; the ranger was too young and too arrogant to be prudent, and too vocal to be trustworthy. He much preferred Sir Beren, who was largely silent, unless he had something wise to say. He would even have accepted Bjorn, for Bjorn had a child-like mind, and was pleasant company, always helpful and polite. But he had a bad feeling about the ranger.

He could forgive that Dante was talkative. The noble-boy, as Bobert had deemed him, was just that: a boy. And boys speak more than is prudent. Not to mention that Dante had long since proved to Tad that, however young and imprudent in speech he was, he was a fierce, clever, and brave person; not someone you would wish to have against you in a fight.

Cat was a different story. He had quite a large opinion of himself, and not nearly enough to back it up. Tad wasn't sure why Bobert had ever inducted him into the group, but he was not one to question his superiors. There was no denying that Cat was good with a bow, but his ineptitude at most every other weapon made him, in Tad's mind, a liability, more in need of protection than an asset in the protecting.

Tad sat contemplating all these things, for Tad was a contemplative mind. After a few hours of contemplating these and many other contemplatable things, while also watching and memorizing every movement of the patrols below, he turned, and woke Sir Beren for his watch. He shook his head to indicate that nothing had happened, and laid down to sleep, still contemplating the contemplatable contemplations which he had contemplated up until this point, until he fell asleep with such contemplations on his mind.

The next morning was as silent as the night. Tad rose to find Sir Beren had dug a hole fire, which produced little to no smoke, and had cooked some fresh meat on it. Tad warmed two of his biscuits on the fire, and they had a warm meal to drive out the memory of the damp night. Tad went to the edge of the ridge, and looked down into the valley in the morning light.

The only thing which stood out now, that he had not noticed the night before due to the dark of the night, was a gigantic cart on wheels, which was in its own little courtyard off of one of the roads, and which had no sort of light source around it. Though he could see no occupants, he guessed that the cage held prisoners of war, which meant that it likely held a few from the monastery.

He turned to say as much to Sir Beren, and found he was not there. Tad stood in a panic, worried that Sir Beren would try to attack the camp single-handedly. Rightly so, for Sir Beren was sneaking through the woods towards the camp. Unfortunately, Sir Beren could not see the patrol that was nearly upon him, just as the patrol was blissfully unaware of the interloper they were about to stumble upon.

For the briefest second, Tad was frozen by indecision. He could not simply let Sir Beren be taken unawares by the patrol, and see him either captured or slain. But his only other option would be to intervene directly, and draw the attention of the scouts away from Sir Beren and towards himself. Neither option was pretty, but the right choice was clear.

Tad crashed through the trees with his sword drawn, yelling a war cry of unintelligible nonsense. The patrol turned to find Tad burst into their midst dealing death. Tad fought with the ferocity of the cornered, and several of the Lizards fell before him. Soon, however, the shock had worn off and the Lizards surrounded Tad, prodding at him with their spears. Sir Beren, who, coming to his senses, had taken cover when he heard the war cry, and searched for its source, happened upon the scene of the battle just as a Lizard wrested the sword from Tad's hands. Tad locked eyes with Sir Beren just long enough to relay an unspoken message: Return to Bobert, report the size of the camp.

Tad was dragged bodily down the road by two Lizards, kicking and screaming all the way, until a third smashed him on the head with his helmet, which had fallen off in the struggle, and he fell silent and limp. Sir Beren waited until they were out of sight, and set off in the other direction, back toward the monastery and Bobert, a growing pain in his soul at the painful cost of his foolish mistake.

Dante and Bjorn were walking down a hall. Dante hadn't heard anything else, and had begun to think himself silly and jumpy. As they walked, Bjorn leading the way through the maze of hallways which seemed to stretch endlessly in every way, Dante examined anything and everything he could, hoping to find some secret lever or hatch. Instead, all he found was dust and more dust. It seemed to him that they were getting into a section of the monastery that was not often used. Dante didn't think that they were likely to find this secret somewhere that the monks didn't often go. If he was guarding a secret, after all, he would check it every so often to ensure it was safe.

"Bjorn?" he said, to get the other's attention.

"Yes, Dante Friend?" Bjorn rumbled out, stopping and turning sharply so that Dante ran into him. "Strange time to hug, little companion, but if you insist."

He went to wrap Dante in an all-encompassing hug, and looked confused when Dante danced away and sighed in exasperation.

"No, amico, I do not wish to hug. You stopped too quickly, I did not expect you to stop."

"Sorry, Dante Friend. Why did you say my name?'"

"Because, I do not think we are in the right area. It seems to me that the secret will be in a section oft traveled, no?"

Bjorn screwed his eyes up for a moment in contemplation, and then gave a very decisive nod. "Then let's look for a road traveled more oftly-like. Just one question."

"Sì?" Dante asked, as he looked down adjoining hallways for some disturbance of the dust.

"What does this Oft look like?"

Cat woke to a frowning Bobert inches from his face. With a screech and a leap which, due to his being in a reclined position, was more of a swift backwards scuttle, he was on his feet and quite irate, mostly because Bobert merely laughed and returned to cooking some unknown but quite delicious smelling meat on a fire in a hole that mysteriously produced no smoke.

"Good morning, Cat. Sleep well? You must've. I've been up since dawn. That was, by my count, three hours ago. In the time that I've been waiting for you to rise, I have made use of the ridge to scan for other Lizards. I found none. That used up one hour, if you include my using the height to determine our exact position in relation to the monastery. I scouted the area, and managed to find a few large worms under a log, which I am now cooking. I then returned, made this fire, and cleaned up the last traces of Lizards in the area as best I could. Then I decided I would just wake you up myself, since you seem so intent upon your beauty-rest."

Cat shifted uncomfortably. He wondered how Bobert managed to rise consistently with the dawn, and if he could learn the skill. He also wondered how Bobert had made a fire that produced no smoke. He peered into the hole, was assaulted by a blast of hot air, and quickly withdrew his head, his eyes watering. Bobert began to laugh.

"They didn't teach you about the hole fire during your training?"

"I've just never seen one in person," Cat said, hoping he sounded at least somewhat convincing.

"You didn't build one at the academy? I really must complain to Gramps. You said you were fresh, but you didn't say you were half-trained."

Cat tried to salvage the situation. "I learn better on the job anyway, I've always felt. I'll just learn as we go."

Feeling Bobert's piercing look on his back, he walked around the fire to get a grip on how it worked. It appeared to be a simple hole in the ground, with a fire in the bottom made of small wood and twigs, and a sloping tunnel that opened a few inches from the hole. Cat guessed that it worked by suction: as the fire burnt, a vacuum was formed that drew air through the tunnel, allowing the fire to burn hotter, thus producing less smoke. When combined with the use of only twigs, Cat could see how the fire would produce no smoke, but lots of heat, if fed frequently.

He turned, and saw that Bobert no longer seemed to be watching him. He strolled to the top of the ridge, a brisk morning hike that cleared the last vestiges of sleep from his mind, and surveyed the landscape. He could not say for the life of him which way they had come. Every way but back looked much the same to him, and only back looked different due to the distant mountains. Up on the ridge the wind whipped with a frenzy, and seemed to whisper menacingly.

"*Death...*" the wind seemed to whisper. "*Destruction...*"[12]

---

[12] You might be reading this, thinking that if the wind was whispering death and destruction at you, you would freak out. Not so with Frogs. You see, we live on a world with a quite polite wind, which likes to play in branches and occasionally howls, but which admittedly throws terrible temper tantrums which take Dorothy all the way to Oz.

Frogs, however, live on a world with a quite impolite wind. On a good day, their wind will call them a few rude names, such as Lizard-tongued

BOBERT AND THE WARLORD

The wind picked up, and its whisper grew, becoming more solid, more menacing.

"*So you think that you have won?*" The wind in the trees was like cruel laughter. "*We shall see about that!*"

With renewed vigor the wind caught at Cat, and with a cry he stumbled and fell, and found that no ground was there to catch him. He flung out his arms. His fingers found something, something hard and rough. He grabbed at it, but found no purchase. He was falling, falling, the wind whipped about him and tore at his clothes. His leg scraped against something, ripping his pants and cutting his leg, and desperately he grabbed at it. His hand found something round, and with an arm-jolting yank his fall was suddenly arrested.

He was hanging one-armed, quickly rectified to two-armed, by the root of a tree that was sticking out the cliff face. He had fallen some twenty feet, and still more than that was below him in a sheer drop onto hard ground. Bobert was below, calmly assessing the situation. As he took in the situation through his fear- and adrenaline-soaked mind, Cat felt his grip on the root slipping thanks to the morning dew. He glanced down once more to ask Bobert to hurry, but could not find him. So, gritting his teeth and praying to any deity that happened to care, he put hand over hand and pulled himself a little further up the root. His plan backfired, and he instead slid a little further down. He began to carefully probe out with his feet, trying to find the cliff face, and thus get some support besides the treacherous root, but he swiftly ceased this as well, for he found nothing and slipped further down.

A rope fell a few feet from him, and Bobert's head appeared over the edge.

"Stop wriggling, or I'll be having pancake for breakfast."

Cat did *not* appreciate the humor of the situation.

"You'll need to grab the rope. Grip the root with your knees, so that you can lean out and reach the rope."

Cat tried this, but merely slipped further down. With a jolt of his heart Cat realised that he had run out of root. He froze, and looked up at Bobert with pleading eyes.

---

or scale-backed. On a positively happy day, the wind will merely shout for you to get off his air. On a bad day, however, it is not uncommon for the wind to tell people to die.

"Okay, that's not gonna work. Just hold on." Bobert for once looked worried.

This did not give Cat much hope.

"Are you sure?" He said. "Perhaps if I leap out and spread my arms I can glide to the ground."

"You'll glide for a short distance, certainly. The trouble is pulling out of said glide before you're flattened like a pie crust. I want pie now. I can swing the rope, but not close enough for you to grab. Not and keep it there. You'll have to leap to catch it."

Cat went green at the thought of flying through the air so high above the ground. "Is there no better way?"

Bobert sighed.

"Sure. Let me just get the rescue crew up here to lower me down so I can put a harness on you,' he answered bitingly. 'No, there's no better way! Leap man! Show some backbone!"

Cat gritted his teeth, tensed his muscles, and leapt from the root, grasping for the rope…

Dante and Bjorn had succeeded in finding a path more oft traveled, though Dante had *not* succeeded in explaining to Bjorn that it was a path more oft traveled, not a path that Oft traveled more. Bjorn seemed convinced that Oft was a person, and that they were looking for him, though he couldn't fathom why[13].

Dante had taken the lead this time, walking down a hallway deep in the bowels of the monastery. He had a feeling that they were in the right place, for though this path seemed to be traveled at least

---

[13] It is neither fair, nor quite accurate, to say that Bjorn was unintelligent. In fact, though Bjorn was not more intelligent than most, nor was he much less. He was only slightly below average. He had, however, a very child-like mind, and a very practical mind. He did not understand sarcasm, most humor, or complicated sentences. He also had a smaller vocabulary than Dante due to an educational difference, and often did not understand his friend's bigger or less common words, which Dante only knew because he had been raised in higher society. Often, when Bjorn did not understand a word, he would assume that it was a person.

weekly, by his guess[14], all of the hallways which branched off of it or the places where the path turned into a new hallway were still undisturbed, implying a very specific, well known route. So they followed the path, until it seemed to peter out.

Dante stopped and looked around, confused. There were no doorways nearby. There were no displays. The alcoves were all empty. The one to his left featured a painting of the Light One's Fire, which had burnt the forests of the world and left them clean for the Light One's followers to repopulate.

The one to his right, on the other hand, featured the Light One, who was depicted as a strange sort of slightly pink, fleshy creature that had black fur only at the top of his head and around his mouth. He was quite humongous, more than three times the size of the prophet he held in his hand, and was obviously quite displeased, for he bared all of his hideously white teeth, and held his other hand in a fist, with the thumb sticking up.

As Dante inspected the strange painting of The Light One, he noticed that, where The Light One's elbow came to the edge of the alcove, there was a dark discoloration. Thinking it a shame for dirt to ruin such a beautiful, admittedly strange painting, he went to rub it away, and his thumb found not dirt, but rusted metal. Surprised, Dante inspected the metal, and found another piece nearer the top and one nearer the bottom.

"Why would builders put metal in an alcove?" Dante asked Bjorn, confused.

"Maybe," Bjorn postulated, "They couldn't get the metal out of the way, so they built around it?"

"That would only work if this alcove was built after the rest of the monastery, though. And then there is the question of why there would be metal at the edge of a half-built alcove, no?"

Bjorn smiled a smile he rarely smiled. He smiled a eureka smile. "What if the alcove is not an alcove?"

---

[14] Dante had an incredible knowledge of dust patterns. Growing up in a huge, empty house which had a team of maids to clean it and who were paid extra to entertain him, he had learned quickly to read the dust pattern, so that he could know where the maids went the least and thus where he could most effectively hide.

AS TRANSLATED BY KERLESS HOPPS

Dante looked at his friend in confusion. "Whatever do you mean, amico?"

Bjorn looked confused again. "Don't know. But you said an alcove wouldn't have metal. And this has metal. So this isn't an alcove?"

Dante looked surprised, and proud. "Fine logic, amico. Quite solid Aristotelian[15] reasoning from you, I must say. Where you learned it I couldn't begin to fathom, but you are quite right, sì. This is no alcove. In fact, thanks to your reasoning, I have had an idea of my own. I would hazard a guess that it is a door, and these metal bits are the hinges. Do the honors, signore?"

Bjorn stepped forward, and placed his right hand on the back of the alcove. His muscles strained, and rippled, and the back of the alcove exploded away from him.

"I do not think it was a door, Dante Friend," the Giant rumbled. "It wouldn't open."

"I think they blocked an old doorway," Dante answered, examining the small hall that Bjorn had unwittingly punched in the alcove. "We might as well finish what we have begun. Please, signore, break the rest of it down."

Bjorn looked at Dante scandalized, and gestured to the illustration of The Light One.

"But Dante-Friend," he said, "I can not destroy a picture of the Holy One. Mamma would be mad!"

Dante smiled his most soothing smile, and patted Bjorn on the arm. "My friend, what is done is done, and look how you have already broken half of his face. A picture is not The Light One, thankfully, and I doubt he will mind much should we accidentally harm a poor imitation."

---

[15] My readers of the more human persuasion may, of course, be wondering how Frogs are aware of Aristotelian reasoning. The answer is quite simple, though it does involve a freak accident with an inter-dimensional portal, and the lucky wanderings of a Frog who quickly changed his name to Aristoadle and got rich pretending to understand logic.

BOBERT AND THE WARLORD

Bjorn looked doubtful for a moment, before nodding hesitantly and turning back to the alcove. He peered through the hole, and then expanded it by grasping the edges and breaking them off like chunks of cookie. Once he had finally expanded the hole enough for a body to fit through, Dante took a torch and led the way into the small room beyond.

The wall's of the room were a panoramic painting depicting the armies of The Light One fighting the armies of some horrible being, which was depicted as a vague mass of black clouds. The Light One battled the Dark in the middle of the field, and appeared to be winning, though he seemed to be much weakened. Throughout the battlefield were four other figures, clearly painted, one red, one green, one black, and one white. Each of them seemed to be commanding a legion of the Dark One's army, though each legion was different. The red figure was leading an army of Lizards and other such well-known barbaric races, ill-equipped but ferocious, ripping into the Light One's armies with fang and claw as much as with their weapons. The green figure was leading what appeared to be a legion of half decayed corpses, which flung the opposing soldiers with unnatural strength, or tore them limb from limb. The black one seemed to be leading a legion of half-starved creatures, ranging from emaciated snakes to starving Frogs, which feasted on the fallen and living as though driven by abysmal hunger. The white figure was at the front of an endless legion of what appeared to be Locusts, that pestilent race which had long menaced Frogan society.

The Light One's armies, on the other hand, were composed of the civilized races: Frogs of every sort from every corner of the world, tree and toad alike, from rainforest and desert; Praying Mantises, adorned in the armor of the Light One's holy orders,, and wielding their serrated claws as weapons in themselves; Turtles served as war beasts, carrying companies of soldiers deep into the Enemy's armies; even some Lizards fought on the Light One's side, enlightened enough to see the flaw in their people's barbaric ways.

The room was adorned with nothing but this painting, and in the middle a pedestal, on which was a book. Dante approached the book cautiously, keeping a sharp eye out for traps, but finding none. Feeling slightly foolish for actually expecting booby-traps, he reached the pedestal, and looked at the book.

The book had a bright cover, which featured a small Frogan child playing on the cover. The child played with a doll, hugging it, and behind her smoke was coming from the chimney of a picturesque cottage, the windows of which were awash with candlelight. A mountain was in the background, and a stream which reflected the red of the setting sun ran down from it and past the cottage. In the field on the other side of the stream a Frog was spread out asleep, and little creatures played around it. The sun, high in the sky, grimaced at its own brightness, and looked down upon the happy scene.

The first inconsistency Dante noticed was the sun. The sun was high in the sky, even though the water of the stream was red as though it was sunset. With an almost visible shift, the image on the cover of the book seemed to change, and became suddenly much less happy, and much clearer, like a veil had lifted. It was as bright as ever, but now Dante saw a completely different set of images.

A child was indeed on the cover, but this child was being strangled by a doll with fiery eyes. Smoke indeed came out of a cottage, but out of the open windows, which were awash not with candlelight but with roaring fire. The mountain in the background had dark shapes rushing through the woods, boding of death and destruction. The stream reflected not the sunlight, but ran red with blood. And a Frog did lay in the field, but across it rushed small Lizards, which ripped at its flesh and lapped at its blood.

Dante sprang back from the abominable scene with a cry, and Bjorn looked between him and the book in confusion.

"What is it that scares you so, Dante Friend? Books can be intimidating when they are big, but surely they are not so scary as this?"

Dante shook where he stood, and felt a chill come over him. "That is no book, Bjorn. At least not a normal one. Not a good one. É il male... It is evil."

"Yes, it is. I thank you for finding it. I did not enjoy the prospect of searching this entire dreadful place by myself."

Dante whipped around to see a figure, shrouded in robes of blackest night, stooped and malicious. Shorter than Dante by a head, he could tell nothing else of the figure, until it raised its hand and a glint of red light reflected from the torch. Just then there was a sharp flash of light, and everything went black.

BOBERT AND THE WARLORD

Tad sat in a hut in what he guessed was the middle of the war camp. He had kicked and screamed and fought like a maddened cat when the Lizards had caught him, to give Sir Beren some chance to escape undetected, and he had been rewarded for his efforts with a bash on the head from his own helmet. He gingerly reached up and felt the side of his head, wincing at the pain. His fingers came away sticky with warm blood. His mouth felt oddly empty, and after a moment he realized that he could neither taste nor smell. He had hoped that Bobert would rescue him, but now he feared that Bobert would be too slow. Clearly he had a concussion, and if he didn't get attention to his head soon, who knows what could happen? He had seen many stout men fall to seemingly innocuous head wounds in his days in the King's army, and he was not about to join their ranks.

Just as Tad was making himself as comfortable as possible in the sparse hut, gingerly resting his aching head on the softest part of his arms, two Lizards entered with teeth bared. Tad struggled to his feet, and his vision swam as a wave of dizziness washed over him. Before he knew what was happening, the Lizards had leapt forward, and each gripped him firmly by an elbow. The Lizards pushed him towards the door, but his head swam with weakness and his knees buckled under him. One of the Lizards cursed and tried to yank Tad to his feet, but he was simply too weak. In a thickly accented, strange tongue, the Lizard barked at its companion, and together they lifted him by his arms and began to drag him from the hut, his body too weak even to struggle against them. The guards dragged him out of the door of the hut, into a large intersection of paths which they crossed without stopping, and they entered the huge hall which Tad recognized vaguely as the hall he had seen in the midst of the camp the night before, the hall of white wood and dark fur.

The hall, however, was not built out of wood, as Tad had thought, but out of gigantic bones bleached white, at their thickest, easily twice as round as Tad's body. Furs of humongous size, likely from cats and squirrels at least, if not from even larger beasts, were stretched across the bones and tied with huge leather strips of similar origin. The walls were lined with suits of armor, not one of which matched the others, which seemed to be of all sorts of materials and styles. Tad guessed that they were spoils, taken from the peoples and armies that these Lizards had battled over the years. Some of the suits contained guards, who, to the inexperienced eye, would merely look like more suits of empty armor. Tad, however, was not fooled, and he counted at least ten hidden guards.

A row of columns, which appeared to be gigantic leg bones, separated the stolen armor and hidden guards from the rest of the hall. Other Lizards, these normally equipped, stood guard next to the pillars, so few that one who did not know of the hidden guards would assume that the lord of the hall was supremely unconcerned of any danger. The center of the hall contained two rows of big bronze braziers, which burnt a flame redder than red, and cast a light the color of blood. These braziers proceeded in a dual procession next to the columns, on either side of a fancily woven carpet obviously plundered from some wealthy and skilled society.

At the end of this rug sat a throne. The base of the throne was a cat's skull, and the empty sockets of its eyes served as places for the occupant's feet to rest. The throne's back was made from a cat's ribs, set so that they opened forward, forming a half circle, and the arms of the chair appeared to be the cat's tail, curled around, with each end resting upon the ground. At the top of the throne's back was a huge shield, forged to look like a fearsome roaring dragon's head; its eyes were rubies, and in its mouth it held a red diamond carved to look like strikingly realistic flame.

As Tad was dragged into the hall, he noticed these things about the hall, before he was unceremoniously dumped before the empty throne. He pushed himself into a kneeling position, his head ringing and his limbs still weak, and forced himself to glare defiantly at the leader of the Lizards, which emerged from somewhere at the back of the hall, shaking the entire hall with each heavy step as the giant settled to sprawl lazily in the throne.

The Lizard that sat before Tad and regarded him with an unconcerned look was huge; it would have easily towered over Bjorn. Its muscles rippled, and it flexed its long, clawed fingers constantly, as though it longed to snatch Tad up and devour him. It had a short snout and two predatory eyes, blood red. Its lips were pulled back in an evil smile, and it seemed to have an unnatural amount of teeth, all sharp and vicious. The entire length of its back was lined with spikes, all tipped with red, right down to the end of its tail, which lay curled around one of the cat skull's fangs. The Lizard wore thick leather pants, but no armor on its torso, and its fingers were adorned in rings. Its feet had neither boots nor sandals, but were hard and scarred, and it wore neither crown nor helm. When it spoke, its voice was a deep and deadly growl that managed to strike fear even in Tad's stout heart.

"So," said he, "You are the Frog that so foolishly attacked my patrol. Alone, I might add. You killed an impressive amount of them."

He said the last bit with a cold smile, as though the lives of his followers were meaningless, and their deaths only held as much value as they amused him.

"You are smaller than I thought, and rather older. I'd hoped you were that hero I've been warned of, even threatened with. No matter, I suspect that you work with him. This... Bobert, I believe they call him? His armor will make a nice addition to my collection, I hope. And as for you? Well, I have a special plan for you. You were pretty gutsy when you attacked my patrol," Here he leaned forward, and showed every single one of his wicked teeth, "So I think in the end I'll mix yours with his and make myself a nice gut pudding. Hah!"

Bobert held the rope as Cat scrambled onto the cliff ledge and collapsed under the morning sun. As Bobert re-rolled the rope and hung it from his side, he sat down next to Cat. He waited a few minutes to speak, allowing Cat to recover from his shock, and then he asked what happened.

"Well," Cat replied, "I was at the top of the ridge, surveying the landscape, when the wind picked up. It was… almost alive. It's like it talked to me, threatened to throw me off. And next thing I know I'm falling. I'm lucky there was a root there, or I'd be dead now."

Bobert was silent for a minute, deep in thought, before answering.

"I think it'd be best if we left this place, and made our way back to the monastery quickly. I don't like the sound of this voice. It sounds like magic, and I don't like magic."

The two made their way down the ridge, and came back to the campsite. The wind began to pick up as they did so, and blew a cold blast around them. The leaves whipped up and swirled around them in an autumnal dance, and Bobert could feel that a cold front was coming this way.

"We need to go quickly, Cat. I don't like the idea of being caught in this cold after dark. I'd like to sleep between a wall and a fire tonight. You pack up, and I'll ensure that all the coals are out one last time, eh?"

Cat did not respond. He merely caught Bobert by the arm and threw him behind a rocky outcropping in the tree line. Bobert found himself sandwiched between Cat and the rocks as a great cracking rent the forest, followed by a thunderous sound and a blast of dust and small bits of shrapnel which shot through the air, and next a wave of boulders and rocks which split around the outcropping and tumbled into the forest around them. When the noise and chaos died down, Bobert peered over the outcropping to see that the entire cliff face had sheared away, and had come crashing down on the campsite, leaving the ledge a rocky heap. Had Cat not flung them behind the outcropping, both of them would surely now be dead.

"That was quick thinking," Bobert said, "And I thank you. But how did you know that was coming? I have keen ears and was looking at the cliff, and I had no indication."

Cat smiled grimly. "You heard nothing because you were talking. That time the wind definitely said something. It said 'Nice try.'"

Bobert stared at Cat for a minute. "You are sure of this? I can see that you are. Very well. We must go, but not to the monastery. We set out for Croak. If there is a wizard powerful enough to control the winds, to create a rockslide, then Grogory should hear. He can tell us where to look, and what to look for."

Bobert stood up, and looked around.

"I can't be sure," he said, "But from what I remember Croak is that way."

He pointed in a certain direction, and the two of them set out for hearth and home, hopefully.

Bobert sighed a sigh of immense proportions.

There was, naturally, a problem, in the form of a massive gorge with rocky cliffs for walls and no way to cross. It ran as far as Bobert could see either way, with not even a tree fallen across it. It was quite deep, with whitewater at the bottom, and walls worn smooth from decades, perhaps centuries of erosion. Bobert and Cat stood examining the problem, weary already from a morning's hike, with a while yet to go.

Cat spoke first.

"Well, now that we've rested up a bit, let's tackle this gorge, shall we?"

"I thought we already were." Bobert replied dryly.

Cat ignored him, and strolled up and down the side of the gorge, talking to himself.

"None of the fallen trees are tall enough to lay across, and we have neither time nor means by which to chop down a tree that would suit our purposes. So what do we do? Well, let's take stock of our resources.

"We have rope, though it isn't long enough to cross the gorge once, much less twice. So much for a rope bridge. We have… well, that's all we have. Okay. So what's around us? Nature provides, after all.

"We have fallen trees which are too short, and all in varying stages of decomposition, not suitable for crossing anyway. We have… nothing else. Wait, what's that? A vine of some sort. It's strong. Woody, but fairly flexible. Eureka! Bingo! Aha! Any number of other interjections that I could interject here!"

Cat ripped the vine from the tree, until he had quite a length, which he dragged over to the edge of the gorge, while Bobert watched him half in confusion and half in amusement.

"What do you plan to do with that?" Bobert asked, largely because he knew Cat wanted him to.

"I'm going to make a rope bridge. We'll be able to cross on it, and won't have to climb down the gorge, if we even could."

Bobert smiled at the obvious hole in Cat's plan.

"How are you going to secure it on the far side?"

Cat in turn smiled the kind of brilliant smile one would expect from a magician just about to perform a mind-boggling trick.

"Easy. I need your rope."

He rolled an extremely heavy rock onto one end of the vine, and tied the other end of the vine to one of his arrows with the rope. He took aim, and drew the bow as tightly as he could, until it seemed as though the string would snap, and then he released. The arrow whistled through the air like an incredibly irate hornet, until it struck a tree on the other side of the gorge with enough force to drive the arrow in halfway up its shaft. Cat stepped back and proudly examined his handiwork, and when Bobert tested the vine with a foot, it seemed to be fairly sturdy.

"So what now?" Bobert said. "You expect me to shimmy across that thing?"

"Hmm? Oh, no. I'm not done."

"Well get to it then."

Cat took another arrow, and with his own rope tied it to the other end of the vine, which was sticking out from under the rock. He rolled the rock away, and notched the second arrow. This time, he aimed at a nearby tree, quite a few feet above their heads, and shot, sinking the second arrow as far as the first.

The result was a line, strung above the gorge, which sloped steeply, the higher end being the same side they were on. Cat repacked everything he had taken out, and removed his belt. Standing on a boulder to reach high enough up, he slung his belt across the vine and, with the easy confidence of one who does not actually risk his life often, but would have you believe he does, he kicked off, and ziplined across the gorge. He landed on the other side at a run and nearly fell to his knees, but he recovered and turned to give Bobert a sign that he could come.

Bobert sighed again, wondering why he had chosen to travel with Cat, instead of Sir Beren or Tad, and climbed on the boulder. He gingerly tested his weight on the vine, and inspected it closely. Satisfied that it probably wouldn't kill him to cross on it, he slung a belt across it and kicked off from the boulder. About half-way across, he heard a whisper in the wind and a loud crack. He couldn't turn to see what it was, but he didn't have to.

The vine lost all tension, and he was being propelled by pure momentum alone. He hit the gorge hard, the edge hitting him in the midriff with an audible crack. He flung his hands forward and clawed at the ground, getting a grip on some rocks which were sticking up. Cat rushed forward, and grabbed his arms, pulling him up from the gorge.

BOBERT AND THE WARLORD

The pain was excruciating, and Bobert could do nothing but lay on the ground as dark spots danced before his eyes and clouded his vision.

Cat watched him anxiously, until Bobert finally sat up.

"I knew that stupid vine wouldn't work. Why do I ever listen to you?"

Cat shuffled his feet embarrassedly.

"You got across, didn't you? I didn't think the arrow would break after just the two of us."

Bobert tried to stand, but winced and sat back down.

"I got across? I need to be able to walk, and fight. I'm pretty sure you broke my vertebrae, you imbecile."

"Sorry."

"You ought to be. I can't walk like this. Listen to me. I think I know what area of the forest we are in, now. Go into the tree line, and look for a bright blue flower. Bring it to me. Be quick about it."

Bobert pulled himself into a sitting position as Cat hurried off into the trees to follow Bobert's instructions. A few moments later Cat returned, with a small bouquet of bright blue flowers in his hands. He handed them to Bobert, and Bobert crushed them in his palms, until he had a paste. He rubbed this paste over the area that hurt, and then sat back. Though his pain did not subside completely, it did dull enough that he thought he might be able to rise. He gritted his teeth and struggled to his feet. He swayed a little from the pain, but steadied himself, and took stock of the situation.

"We've traveled too far east, thanks to the gorge. But I know where we are now. This gorge marks the border of Croak's territory. We're no more than an hour out. Let's get going. I need a drink."

Bobert sat shirtless in the inn of Croak, letting Amphibia tend his wounds and wrap his midriff in bandages. Instead of the drink that he'd wanted and come in to get, she had insisted upon giving him some strange honey-flavored tea that made his entire body warm and completely got rid of the pain from his midriff.

Cat sat at the other side of the bar, looking thoroughly chastised. When Amphibia had gotten the entire story from a reluctant Bobert[16], she had turned her tongue on Cat like a whip, and had made

---

[16] Bobert was reluctant because, no matter how mad he was about it, no

him thoroughly wish that he had been a better child to his mother. After a solid five minutes of yelling, Bobert had made a noise of pain, partly to remind Amphibia that he needed attention, and partly to save Cat from any more chastisement.

Amphibia, turning back to Bobert, had chastised him shortly for being dumb enough to trust Cat's vine, but had gone easy on him due to the wound and his apparent, though slightly overstated, discomfort. She had bustled around making the tea, and then had demanded he take off his shirt so that she could wrap his wounds. Bobert had complied, knowing better than to try to argue.

Throwing a last venomous glance at Cat, Amphibia finished wrapping Bobert's wounds and helped him put his shirt back on, smoothing out the wrinkles and straightening the edges. Finally she sat down on the stool next to him, and asked him to tell her about all that had happened. She sat patiently through the entire story, only interrupting to remind him to drink his tea. When Bobert was done, she spoke.

"So you've come to ask Grogory about this whispery voice, I suppose? I doubt you'd have come all the way back to Croak just for a drink."

"Maybe I came to see you." Bobert said with a winning smile.

Amphibia glared at Bobert until he rearranged himself gingerly and continued on like he had said nothing.

"Right you are, of course. Only decided to stop in here for a drink, to dull the pain. Whatever's in this tea though, it's made me feel like new. Thanks."

"You're very welcome, of course. Right. Let's go see Grogory."

"We?" Cat asked in alarm.

Amphibia smiled her sweetest smile.

"Oh yes, we. I don't trust you not to get Bobert killed now, so I'll be coming with you."

Cat paled slightly.

---

one deserves to be yelled at by Amphibia like she was known to yell at people who got him hurt.

BOBERT AND THE WARLORD

"But… but we can't…"

Amphibia cut him off.

"I'm coming. Suck it up, buttercup."

Grogory was in his cave, no surprise, working with his books. When Bobert entered, Grogory jumped up with a smile, which became a little uncomfortable at the sight of Amphibia, and completely disappeared at the sight of Cat. Never taking his eyes off of the last, Grogory sidled over to Bobert and whispered quite loudly,

"Who may this be?"

Bobert smiled and introduced Cat, saying, "This is Cat Frills. He works with me now. He is a recent recruit from the Council of Forest Rangers. He's a bit green, but he's pretty clever. He's been a help."

Amphibia laughed scornfully, and with a contemptuous glance at Cat she said, "A help? At what, killing you quicker?"

Bobert threw Amphibia a reproachful look, "As you can imagine, I didn't come down here for a social visit. I need to pick your brain, if you don't mind."

Grogory chuckled nervously. "So long as it doesn't hurt."

Grogory shifted over to his sitting area[17] and folded into his arm chair. Bobert noted that Grogory seemed much more at ease around him now, and had hardly even flinched when Amphibia had spoken earlier. He settled down onto the half-sofa with Amphibia, and was forced to squeeze uncomfortably closer to her when Cat settled down next to him with what he mistakenly thought was a winning smile aimed at Grogory, though it simply looked as though he were contemplating all the ways in which he could murder the little scholar. Bobert rearranged to make himself more comfortable, accidentally stepping on Cat's toes in the process, hissing at him to stop smiling like that.

Grogory began to look uncomfortable, smiling awkwardly back at Cat and at the forced closeness between Bobert and Amphibia, so Bobert decided it would be best if he started with some small talk.

"So, Grogory, have you been busy translating mysterious scrolls and ancient hieroglyphs?"

---

[17] An impressive feat, considering the sitting area was at least a dozen feet away. Only the most skilled of shifters can shift over that great of a distance.

AS TRANSLATED BY KERLESS HOPPS

Grogory looked immensely relieved that Bobert had broken the silence.

"Why yes, actually! A few months ago the Grand Librarian sent me a shipment of scrolls, you know, he was handing them out to notable libraries, and thought mine deserved praise. I am quite proud to have been-"

Cat cut him off. "That's nice, but the time of Cat Frills is far too valuable to waste with uninteresting small talk. We come with purpose. Bobert and I last night tracked down a contingent of Lizards, and slaughtered them. There was blood everywhere. We stayed in that place the night, naturally, to ensure that the fire which we used to burn the bodies did not spread. First light came to find me atop a ridge, surveying the landscape to know what to expect. It is always good to know what to expect, so that you can plan ahead. As I contemplated, a wind came fierce and strong, and it carried on it a voice, whispery and cold, which told me portents of death and destruction, and with a distinct threat blew me off the edge of the cliff. My quick reflexes and quicker mind of course came to my rescue and I grabbed a tree root as I fell, halting my descent, and allowing Bobert enough time to lower a rope. A few minutes later, after Bobert had rested and we made our way down the slope, as we stood under the cliff, I heard again that voice, threatening me once more, and I bodily threw Bobert behind a nearby outcropping of rock, and myself with him, just in the nick of time to save both our lives, for the entire cliff face came loose and came crashing down on the very spot where I had stood seconds earlier. Had I not acted as quickly as I did, both Bobert and I would be bloody heaps under a pile of rocks."

Cat finished his tale with a verbal flourish, and left Grogory sunken in his chair, shivering visibly, and fanning himself with a blank page. Bobert shook his head and opened his mouth to speak, but hadn't made a sound before Amphibia cut him off.

"Oh shut up, you lump! You know perfectly well that half of that was a lie."

Bobert cut in, before she could continue. "Enough bickering, you two. No, Cat, I don't care if you didn't do anything, and besides you did. We came here with purpose, and I am not in a pleasant enough mood to listen to you two."

Cat and Amphibia subsided into tense silence, with Cat glaring at everyone involved and Amphibia pursing her lips so hard they seemed to disappear.

"It didn't happen anything like that," Bobert continued, "But most of what happened doesn't matter. The important details are this[18]: I and my heroes were at some point last night visited by a bloody praying mantis, who begged us to expel the barbarian Lizards from his monastery. Naturally, we agreed. We came to the monastery to find the majority of the Lizards had moved on. Bjorn Giant battled and defeated a Bullfrog they were using as a blunt instrument, and we fought the remaining Lizards. Unfortunately, a large number escaped.

"I didn't wish to see any Lizards escape to reform and attack us from behind, but I also wanted to keep tabs on the rest of the Lizards, and to learn why they were interested in the monastery, so I split us up into three groups. Sir Beren and Tad went to spy on the larger Lizard force, and that's the last I know of them. Dante and Bjorn I told to search the monastery, to discover the reason for the Lizards' interest. Cat and I pursued the escaping Lizards.

"We caught the Lizards under a cliff, and Cat and I took care of them. I'll spare you the gory details. We stayed in that place the night, and next morning I scouted around. I came back and woke Cat a few hours after sunrise, and he at some point felt the need to gaze from the top of the cliff. As he stood up there, he says he heard a voice, and then the wind blew him off. After I had saved him from that predicament, we were walking near the tree line and he apparently heard the voice again, and threw me and himself behind a rocky outcropping, in a moment of quick thinking. Then the entire cliff face comes crashing down. Now, I didn't hear this voice either time, but if Cat says he heard it, then I trust him. And that cliff face was sturdy. It didn't come down by chance.

"I thought it prudent to return here and explain the situation to you, so we set out for Croak. We were hampered in our journey by a gorge, but Cat's inventive thinking secured for us a zipline over it. As I crossed, however, the line broke, and I was injured. What is peculiar is

---

[18] For those of you just joining our program, or following along at home.

that that time, I would swear I too heard a voice in the wind, right before the line broke, and it had been perfectly sturdy when Cat crossed it."

Grogory sat for a moment sunken in his chair, contemplating all he had heard. With piercing eyes he gazed at Cat, and seemed to nod to himself. Eventually, he rose, and, walking to his desk, he wrote a short note, which he tied to the leg of a large insect. He let the insect go, and it whizzed out of the library and off through the tunnels.

"What was that you just sent?" Bobert asked of Grogory.

Grogory shook his head sadly. "Hopefully unnecessary. We should go. I shall be accompanying you for the remainder of this… adventure."

Bobert, Amphibia, and Cat all opened their mouths to protest, but he raised his hands to quiet them and cut them off in a peculiarly soft-spoken yet final manner.

"Distasteful as it is, what you have described to me are worrisome phenomenon. Specifically, I believe that these Lizards have in their employ some sort of a sorcerer. I believe that it would be best if I was there to observe any further phenomena with my own two eyes. Thus, I must go with you. Now, there is no use in arguing further. I shall come with you, or else follow on my own, the latter of which severely lowers the chances of survival for everyone involved, so it would be best not just for me, but for you, to allow me to accompany you, instead of forcing me to follow you."

Dante awoke with a splitting headache. As a matter of fact, all of him ached. He was still in the room, but now the book was gone. The windows in the hallway were no longer black; they were bright with the light of morning. Dante scrambled to his feet, and stumbled over to Bjorn, shaking him awake.

"Bjorn! Bjorn! Awaken! Bjorn!"

The Giant rolled over, and slowly opened his eyes. He sat up, and stretched, filling the entire room, and then suddenly froze as he winced with pain.

"Head hurts. Mean Robe Man made my head hurt!"

Dante strolled out of the room and looked either way down the hallway.

BOBERT AND THE WARLORD

"Sì, and he seems to have bolted. We need to get moving, see if he is still in the monastery."

Bjorn got to his feet and joined Dante in the hallway.

"Which way did Mean Robe Man go?"

Dante examined the dust in the hallways, and then pointed down the way they had come the night before.

"It looks like he followed this path, back towards the main monastery."

The two set off gingerly down the hallway following the trail, which brought them back to the main of the monastery. Dante stepped outside, examining the ground to search for prints, and Bjorn stepped out behind him. The morning air helped to clear the pain from their heads, and the two spent a moment breathing it in, enjoying the stark difference between it and the stuffy air of the monastery.

"What did you find, Dante Friend?"

"The robed figure seems to have left. He set off down the road, towards where Sir Beren and Tad went. È cattivo."

Dante looked up at the sky, and was shocked to find that it was not morning at all. The sun was riding high in the sky, and it was closer to noon than anything else. As Dante's eyes came back down, he happened to see, coming round a bend in the road, Bobert and Cat, accompanied by none other than Amphibia, and some Frog whom Dante did not yet know.

The sun was riding high in the sky by the time that Bobert and his three companions made it back to the monastery. Necessity and a smaller group had allowed them to travel much faster than they had the day before, despite Bobert's wound, which, though soothed by Amphibia's tea, was still sore when he moved. As they came around the last bend in the road, they saw Dante and Bjorn standing at the entrance, squinting into the sun as they watched the approaching party. Cat spoke first, as soon as they were within speaking distance.

"Whatever you have to say can wait, and on our side at least we have plenty to say. But now, I hunger for lunch. Let us go inside out of the sun and eat first, then discuss."

The others did not object to this plan, so they all made their way inside, and ate food which Amphibia almost magically produced from her pack. As they ate, Bobert told his and Cat's tale, and Dante told his and Bjorn's.

"Describe this voice," Grogory interjected, when Dante was finished.

"I am sorry, signore, but who are you? You do not look like a condottieri, nor indeed like any person of note I know."

Bobert, realising that he had forgotten the formalities, made the proper introductions, and then repeated Grogory's question to Dante.

"Well, it only spoke once, but it stuck with me. Strange, it was. Very airy, like a whisper, but perfectly clear, no? I could almost have mistaken it for a malevolent wind in the trees, like you describe. How about you, Bjorn? What did it sound like to you?"

Bjorn looked at Dante in confusion, and said, "What voice, Dante Friend?"

He reached over and tapped on Dante's head with his knuckles. "Did fall knock something loose up there?"

Dante knocked Bjorn's hand away, and said, "No, no, the voice. Sai, right before we were knocked out? The Mean Robe Man's voice?"

Bjorn began to look worried. "Mean Robe Man did not speak, Dante Friend…"

Grogory interjected, before Dante could reply. "Fear not for your sanity, good sir. No doubt your friend could *not* hear this 'robed man', just as Bobert could not. My guess is that he was not speaking, but was magically projecting his voice into your mind."

Bobert growled. He had a notorious hatred for all things magical, and did not like even the mention of it. Despite his overall disinterest in religion, he called all things magical unholy abominations, and claimed that the source of all magic was demons.[19]

"Where did it go?" he asked Dante.

---

[19] This had caused much debate between Bobert and travelling magicians, who sold their skills to solve problems or simply entertain. Many traveling magicians refused to pass through Croak for that very reason, and performances in the town were outright banned by the Magician's Society.

BOBERT AND THE WARLORD

"È cattivo. I do believe that it traveled off in the same direction as Sir Beren and Tad. Hopefully they manage to avoid it entirely, no?"

Bobert stood abruptly, and began to repack his supplies.

"We can't take that chance. We must go after it, recover this book it stole, and ensure that it doesn't get back to the Lizard camp, if at all possible. I don't know what this book is, but if a sorcerer wants it, it can't be good."

The sun was high, the day was hot, the road was long, and Cat would not let them forget it. It got to the point that, had former not been in the very rear, and latter at the very front, Bobert would probably have murdered him, or at least have insured his impending death, by way of removing his arms and tongue. He was nearly ready to go to the back and do so when, in the distance coming down the road towards them, there appeared a figure. They approached cautiously, and after a few more minutes the figure resolved itself into Sir Beren, who stopped and waited for the others.

"Where's Tad?" Bobert asked, when they were close enough to not have to yell.

Sir Beren signaled for them to continue on, fell into step beside Bobert, and told him his tale, of how he had grown wrathful at the Lizards for holding his brethren, how he had begun to recklessly charge the gate, and how Tad had stopped him before he ran headlong into a patrol, allowing himself to be captured and Sir Beren to escape undetected. Sir Beren told all of this to Bobert as they marched onward towards the camp, and then began to describe the camp's layout, defenses, and patrol.

When he was done, Bobert walked on for a while in silence. When finally he spoke, it was in a voice conveying not anger, but great disappointment. Anyone who has experienced both can tell you that, from someone you respect, the latter is far worse.

"You must learn to control your anger, Sir Beren. It could well have cost Tad his life. Learn to control it, or leave my team and return to your peaceful monastery. Apparently they could use strong fighters. But either way, I do not intend to clean up your messes any longer."

Sir Beren looked ashamed of himself. "I will do my best."

For a little while they walked on in silence, until Sir Beren spoke again as though the words burst unwilling from his lips.

"I just get so *angry*. I can't help it. I try to control it, to swallow it, to ignore it, but it just eats away at me until I let it out, and then there's nothing I can do to stop it."

Bobert nodded. "I am not the one you ought to turn to when you need help with emotions, Sir Beren. Surely there is someone you can talk to about this? A monk at your monastery, perhaps?"

"There was," Sir Beren replied, "But I haven't seen him in quite a while, since I was called away to help you. Now I fear that he is held prisoner by the Lizards, if he is even alive. He is quite old, and I fear the life of a prisoner may not agree with him, though our vows of poverty certainly help."

"Fear not, Sir Beren. We shall free all of your brothers, and make these Lizards pay while we're at it."

Again, they marched on in silence, until Bobert shook his head as though to clear evil thoughts, and continued in a matter-of-fact tone.

"In the meantime, tell me, have you seen a figure pass? Robed and hooded?"

"Yes, I did. I knew not whether he was friend or foe, so I hid myself among the bushes until he was long past. It carried a strange bundle, wrapped in many layers of cloth. I noticed because it was incredibly protective of it, and I found that strange. Why do you ask? Should I have tried to stop him?"

"No, certainly not. I would not have you face a sorcerer alone."

So Bobert proceeded to tell the entire story, both the experiences of him and Cat, and of Dante and Bjorn. By the time that all members of the party were caught up on all that had happened to the others, they had arrived at the edge of the Lizard encampment. Sir Beren led them up to the clearing that he and Tad had stayed in the night prior, and Bobert began to examine the camp.

A few minutes passed in silence, until Bobert spoke.

"We shall go in at night. It will be easier to get in undetected under the cover of darkness, though we must bear in mind that some of our enemies may see well even in the darkness. Besides that, the only problem is that those walls aren't easily penetrable. In fact, I'm not sure I could get over one alone. It seems as though we'll have to force our way through a gate, in which case we need darkness so that we'll be undetected until we are right up on the gates. If they close them, we'll be locked out for good, and they'll tighten their security all the way around."

Grogory raised a tentative hand. "Forgive me, Bobert, but I believe I have a better plan. When General MacFroggert needed to take a certain city, I recall reading in his memoirs that he had his men strip the uniforms from the enemy soldiers they had captured, and don them. They entered the city under the guise of a scattered band of soldiers that had managed to escape the slaughter. That night, they killed the guards and opened the gates, allowing General MacFroggert to enter and seize the city while most of the enemy soldiers were still asleep."

Cat cocked his head to one side. "But we have no prisoners, and even if we did, they'd notice we're not Lizards."

Grogory smiled a strange, discomforting smile. "No, but there are plenty of patrols in the area. You could attack one of them, kill the Lizards, and take their armor. I noticed one of the patrols down below, and they wear a lot of clothes. I think we could get through the gate unnoticed, if we were careful."

They all carefully contemplated this plan, until Dante tentatively raised his hand.

"Just talk, Dante, this isn't a schoolroom," Bobert said with a sigh.

"Well," Dante replied, "I was just wondering how we get back out with Master Tad? I doubt that they shall merely let us pass with a prisoner."

Everyone turned to Grogory expectantly, but Bobert spoke first.

"That's why we all have to go in. We're gonna have to fight our way out."

The uniforms were tight and heavy, stuffy, constricting, and any other uncomfortable descriptor you might wish to add to the list. They likely all apply.

The uniforms consisted of heavy leather vests with small metal plates stitched to them. The leather vambraces which protected their arms were studded with sharp metal spikes, and were more weapon than armor. A chainmail skirt, leather greaves, and long leather boots protected their lower halves. That was only the armor, however. For some unimaginable reason, the Lizards felt the need to wear a light fabric over most of their bodies. There was a skirt over the chainmail which went down to mid-calf, and a shirt, the sleeves of which went down to the wrist, and tucked into the gloves. Although the cloth completely covered their bodies, it breathed incredibly well, and in fact made them feel somehow cooler, but let neither dust nor eye penetrate it. The strangest part was the headdress that the Lizards wore, which consisted of a single long strand of cloth, wrapped around their heads many times, and which dipped down under their chins, and with the end covered their faces like a veil. Though it was much too confusing for any of the others to understand, Grogory appeared to have studied them before, for he knew exactly what he was doing, and showed the others how to wrap their own.

It took them several minutes to change out of their armor and put all of their own on. Dante and Bjorn, however, were not dressed in this fashion. They retained all of their own armor, and concealed their weapons on their persons, for Bjorn was much too big to disguise as one of the Lizards, and Dante too lean to keep the armor on him.

When they were all finally outfitted properly, concealing their personal weapons about their person if they were too conspicuous, they hid all of their armor and clothing in the campsite, and began the descent to the road a good distance from the gate, to appear as though they were coming from the monastery. The hands of Dante and Bjorn were loosely tied together to make them appear as prisoners, and they walked in the middle of the group.

When they reached the gate, Bobert, who had been walking in the front of the group, was inspected by one of the Lizard guards. One peered suspiciously around the group, and then addressed Bobert.

"Why are your veils up, scum? No sand in this place."

Bobert, without missing a bit, did his best, luckily a very good, impression of a Lizard.

"No sand, but still plenty of sun. Been walking all day, got hot. One idiot collapsed, so I stuck him and had the others put their veils up. These two destroyed most of our water yesterday night, but we woke and captured 'em, we did," he finished by nodding sharply at Dante and Bjorn.

BOBERT AND THE WARLORD

The Lizard peered around at the group again, and then got uncomfortably close to Bobert. His breath smelled ripe and rotten., and Bobert felt it warm and moist on his face, even through the veil.

"So why your veils still up? You're here now. Take 'em down," he turned around and barked at the others in Bobert's group. "Now! All of ya."

Bobert held his hand up in a fist, and then got closer to the guard, dropping his voice to a menacing hiss.

"Now you listen here. These ain't your men. They're mine. And they don't drop their veils unless *I* tell 'em to. Now, you wanna question me? You want *me* to drop my veil? You just ask. But I promise, you *won't like* what's on the other side. Cause just as soon as I report to the boss, and explain to him why I took so long bringin' him some pretty new prisoners, he's gonna send me down here to deal with you as I like, and that *won't* be pretty. *Not one bit.*"

With blinding speed, Bobert pulled out a vicious looking knife and pinned the guard's veil to the gate. Then he pushed the gate, which was slightly ajar from the guard walking through it, all the way open with his foot, the guard stumbling backwards with it, and walked through it with complete confidence. The others broke neither rank nor composure in passing through the gate after him, and Dante and Bjorn played the role of prisoner terribly convincingly.

They passed through the gate and found themselves on a long, straight avenue, with hundreds of tiny, chaotic paths branching off of it to travel through the thousands of tents which were set up without rhyme or reason. From Sir Beren's previous description, Bobert knew that he and his men were on one of the roads which ran to the center of the camp. When they got far enough away from the gate that they could speak without being overheard, Bobert turned to the others.

"Amphibia, Grogory, you're with me. We're going to check out this cage, and then the hall. Dante, Bjorn, you two find an empty tent off the road and hide. Light a fire to show us where you are. We don't need you causing a ruckus, and someone is bound to realize if you walk around the entire camp as prisoners. Sir Beren, Cat, you two go looking for Tad. We, that is Amphibia, Grogory, and I, will search the cage, and that side of the camp. You search the other. We'll meet back at Dante and Bjorn's tent. Understood?"

AS TRANSLATED BY KERLESS HOPPS

When everyone had confirmed that they understood their instructions, he, Amphibia, and Grogory departed, traveling towards the center of the camp at a swift pace which was just slow enough to be inconspicuous. They crossed by means of a variety of pathways and a good sense of direction to one of the other roads, without passing through the central courtyard, and found themselves on what Bobert believed to be the right road for finding the cage.

Soon enough Bobert, Grogory, and Amphibia found what they were looking for. The tents, which had been staked thick as a forest up to that point, ceased suddenly like a hedge in a wide circle, in the center of which was an enormous rolling cage made purely of metal, the back half of which was covered in large rushes. Bobert approached the cage cautiously, hoping not to startle any of the unseen occupants, and cause a panic which would bring down suspicion on him and the others. However, as Bobert approached the cage, and the back half came into view, he realised that it was not occupied by Praying Mantes or Frogs, or indeed even by Lizards. No, what occupied this cage was large, black scaled, and sleek. Bobert could not see its face, for it was curled up away from the light, but he had seen it enough in his nightmares to know what this beast was, just from its muscled body and scaly hide.

"You," he breathed, hardly believing it could be true. Before him lay the creature which he had first encountered deep in the den of the necromancer, that infernal beast of cat and snake, brewed in the devilish concoctions of that unholy sorcerer. Driven off by Amphibia's deep-piercing arrows, Bobert had assumed the abomination had fled far from Croak, to some distant land where it could reign terror on a more complacent people. Yet now he came to find it, captured in the camp of a Lizard warlord.

The Beast's body tightened at the sound of his voice, and slowly, almost scaredly, it raised its head, and turned to look at him. Grogory squeaked and fell backward, Amphibia gasped in shock, and even Bobert's iron stomach turned over.

The Beast's visage was lined with hundreds of scars, some of them freshly opened. It had whip marks crisscrossing all over its face, under the jaw and around the eyes. Its left eye appeared to have been caught by the whipping, and the wound was red and irritated. It's face, vaguely snakish, but with much harder lines lined with spikes of varying sizes, was thinner than when last Bobert had seen it, but it had grown. Its body was easily twice the size of a large snake now, and its two muscled forearms, which ended in long claws, were about half the width of its body. Its wings, though still folded, were quite a bit larger, and could be easily discerned from its body. Its tail trifurcated near the end, and each trifurcation ended in a wickedly sharp barb.

The Beast watched Bobert coldly, suspiciously, but it did not dare attack; it seemed mortally afraid of anyone on the other side of the bars. Bobert backed up slowly, unsure of what would trigger the Beast, and joined Amphibia and Grogory at the edge of the circle. After affirming to his colleagues that it was indeed the Beast, and that it was being forced to act, he guessed, as a beast of war, they moved away, infuriated, but not forgetful of their mission.

They began to search the camp methodically, starting at one end and working their way through, but they had only gotten a third of the way through when they were approached by a large group of Lizards, led by a menacing looking officer.

"What are you three doing?" the officer asked, his voice more hiss than words.

Amphibia and Grogory both looked at Bobert, and he stepped forward to address the officer.

"We are searching for our tent, sir. We lost it."

The soldiers behind the officer chuckled, and he smirked.

"Lost your tent, did you? You must be real fools to lose something that big. Might find it easier, if you took your veils down. Go on."

"Just a bit hot, sir." Bobert shifted uncomfortably.

"Now." The officer's voice left no room for argument.

When Bobert made no move to remove his veil, the officer stepped forward and ripped it off. His smirk grew wider, as he signaled for his men to encircle and take the three. Before Bobert could reach his sword, both Amphibia and Grogory were seized, and there were multiple swords to his throat.

"Do not fight, little hero, or your friends will die on your behalf. And do not worry. You are to be reunited with all of your friends soon. The Warlord will see you now."

The Lizards deposited the captured hero and his allies in the courtyard before the central hall of bone and fur. With cruel smiles and menacing laughs, they poked and prodded until Bobert led his friends into the hall, where his four other companions were already gathered. Dante and Cat were in fairly basic restraints, their hands tied behind their backs and their weapons stript from them. Sir Beren, however, was more tightly bound; instead of rope he was in chains, in shackles not merely around his wrists, but around his ankles as well, and connected between. Bjorn was also bound by chains, thick and heavy ones strapped to each arm and leg, held by five Lizards to a limb.

As they entered the hall, Amphibia and Grogory were taken to the side to join the rest of their company, but Bobert was ushered onward by the sharp prod of a Lizard's spear in the small of his back. He was pushed on, past the many-armored guards who stood half-hidden among the Warlord's trophies, until he was at last before the throne of bone.

On this throne sat the most massive Lizard that Bobert had ever seen. Several heads taller than Bjorn, the Warlord had rippling muscles and a lazy demeanor, sitting flopped in its chair as though the whole thing bored it. It regarded Bobert with a sharp eye, however, and did not seem at all surprised to see him. When it spoke, its voice reverberated through the air like boulders grinding together.

"So, you are the hero? I've been expecting you, though I'd hoped you would be bigger. No matter. You will die all the same." The Warlord turned to his guards. "Execute him, and all his friends. Bring their heads back. They shall march before us on the spears of our forerunners, when we pillage their little village before moving to the next."

As the Warlord leaned back and closed its eyes, the guards marched forward, wresting the Frogs from the hall. But as two Frogs began to drag Bobert backwards, he shirked their grips and leapt forward.

"Wait! I demand to speak."

The Warlord opened one eye, and looked at him with some amusement.

BOBERT AND THE WARLORD

"You have no rights, and no room to make demands. But you do have guts. I'll listen. What do you want?"

Bobert locked eyes with the Warlord, and gathered his courage.

"I want to stake the lives and freedom of my friends and myself against your life, and the surrender and peaceful removal of your people. I want trial by combat."

For a moment a deadly silence settled on the camp, as every eye turned to the giant. Suddenly, a deep and booming laughter erupted from the Warlord's monstrous maw, echoing through the hall and reflected by the cruel laughter of its many followers.

"You want trial by combat, little Frog? Then you shall have it."

With a lazy flick of its hand, the Warlord motioned for its guards, and they led Bobert out of the hall, along with the rest of their prisoners. They took the southern road out of the camp, and all the Lizards they passed seemed to know what was happening, for they fell in behind the prisoners with a sense of expectancy. The Warlord could be heard, strolling behind lazily, but Bobert didn't dare look back to see what was happening. The guards took him out of the camp, and on through the woods, upon a well worn track. They walked for several minutes, until the camp was long out of sight, before they finally came to a vast clearing, which was shaped like a natural arena, with steep dirt walls and a large floor.

The Lizards spread out around the clearing, standing at the edges and hissing as Bobert was brought into the middle and unchained. His sword was pushed into his hands, and the guards retreated. He turned, expecting to see the Warlord enter the arena to fight him, but instead he found the Warlord sitting on a throne at the end of the arena, which appeared to have been built there merely for its pleasure, and from which it smiled a sardonic, almost lazy smile.

"Come down here and fight me, coward!"

The Warlord only laughed at Bobert's taunt, and gestured around the audience.

"Why? I have all these faithful followers, who would love to kill you for my pleasure. But no, I have a special surprise for you. An old friend."

Bobert guessed the 'old friend' that the Warlord referred to was the Beast, and wanted to avoid that particular fight.

"You can't do that. I challenged you."

The Warlord merely smirked a vicious smirk.

"On the contrary, little Frog. The rules of trial by combat specifically state that a ruler may choose a champion from among his or her people to carry out the combat, if they are challenged. I am a ruler, and I choose my champion. I may be large, strong, and evil, but do not make the mistake of assuming that I am stupid."

The Warlord gestured to the other side of the arena, and Bobert turned around, just in time to see the Beast enter with an honor guard of Lizards. What shocked him, however, was not the Beast, nor the Lizards, but the Beast's rider.

Upon the back of the Beast was a Frog tall and regal. Red armor reflected the moonlight as the Beast half-slithered, half-pulled itself into the arena. In one hand the Frog held a small, iron-bound wooden shield, decorated with scenes of bloodshed, pillaging, and war. In his other hand, the Frog held a long spear, with a blood-stained shaft and a crimson tip. The Frog's helmet was opened on the front in a wide T, and Bobert could see glowing red eyes within.

The Beast pulled itself entirely into the arena, and the Lizards around it carried a huge chain to a gigantic stone pillar which stood at one side of the arena. Bobert prepared to face it with a sinking stomach. His foe, however, looked first to the Warlord, paying not even the slightest amount of attention to Bobert. The Warlord raised its hand, and very dramatically pointed its thumb downward, and the Frog immediately focused on Bobert, and caused the Beast to leap at him.

Bobert dodged to the side, and came up on his feet, knowing that even the slightest mistake would cost him his life. Not only did he face the Beast's killer instinct, but it was immediately clear that the rider of the Beast had a killer instinct of his own, and a skill to match. Bobert dodged and the Beast struck, the rider pulled the reins, and when Bobert got too close, he was warded off once more by the rider's deadly spear.

It was a deadly dance where a mistake meant death. Bobert and the Beast danced under the instruction of their deadly conductor, the red-armored rider of the Beast. With a slight twist of his reins the deathly knight could send Bobert scurrying one way or the other. With a jab of his spear he could cause Bobert to leap backwards or to fling himself out of the way. The rider's skill on its own did not surpass Bobert's, perhaps, but when combined with the pure, brutal hatred of the Beast, it wove a deadly net that sought constantly to trap Bobert in its morbid embrace. The dance was weaved, the dancers set in motion, and Bobert could do naught but his part. So while the deadly conductor tugged the reins to and fro, and slashed up and down, in and out with his crimson spear, Bobert dodged and weaved, leapt and stumbled.

But not fast enough.

The air whipped around him as pain exploded throughout Bobert's body, first in his gut and then in his back, and he hit his head with an ear-ringing, head-splitting pain. Dirt clogged his mouth and forced itself down his throat, and for the briefest moment he lay, dazed. But it could not last, for he saw through the cloud of dust that his falling had made, one of the Beast's massive paws slamming down towards him. He rolled desperately to the side, scrambled to his feet, and stumbled through the dizziness away from his foe, brandishing his sword as he turned.

He only saw it this time for the briefest second before it struck, but it was enough time for him to prepare himself. This time, when the Beast slammed it's trifurcated tale into Bobert's midriff, he wrapped one arm around despite the excruciating pain, and with the other stabbed his foe in the tail. He flew through the air as the Beast tried to flick him off, and grinding his teeth against his body's many protests, using the Beast's own ridges as hand-holds, he pulled himself further up, abandoning his sword in favor of the dagger concealed in his boot.

He leapt quickly along the tail of the Beast, and though its rider knew he was there, before the Frog could turn to fight, Bobert was upon him, slashing with his dagger at the leather strips that held him into the saddle behind the Beast's forearms. He dragged the Frog out by the front of his armor, and as the two wrestled they lost their footing, and tumbled one and the same from the Beast's back to the ground below.

Freed of the oppressive weight of its rider, the Beast looked fearfully at the Lizards around the clearing, but none of them moved forward to stop it. Realising with a joy that it had no master, the Beast leapt from the ground, trying to flee while it was free.

Too late it remembered the chain around its neck, and with a jerk it was stopped as the chain pulled taut between it and the stone pillar. It crashed to the ground with earth-shaking force, and Bobert had to roll to the side to avoid one of its tails. The hero leapt to his feet, and was met immediately by the dark-spirited rider, who had cast aside his spear in favor of a massive, bloody flail with a red-stained ball. With its fearsome blows and relentless attack, the rider forced Bobert back until his retreat was checked by cold stone.

The red of the rider's eyes seemed to glint maliciously, flaming with anger. He swung the flail over his head to gain momentum, and brought it down towards Bobert's body, with such force that it seemed to blur. Bobert rolled forward to avoid the blow, and the flail crashed into the stone pillar. Bobert came to his feet and turned, to see that the flail had hit the stone pillar so hard it had shattered, and had run a crack all the way from the top to the very bottom, directly through where the chain was hooked to it. With a ferocious yank of the chain the Beat freed itself, pulling the hook out of the pillar and spreading its wings, spraying the Lizards with its acid-like venom as it raised itself above the tree line, and laboriously flew away.

Bobert, however, did not have much time to watch this, for the rider, his flail shattered, approached Bobert now with a sword drawn from his side, as crimson and blood-stained as his first two weapons, and the two met with a flurry of blows. Yet on the ground, even with the anger that drove him, the rider was no match for Bobert's skill in the sword. Within moments the crimson sword flew from the rider's grip, and with a few well-placed blows the Warlord's champion was brought to his knees. Bobert gripped the rider's helmet, intent to look at the face of the Frog he was to deal judgement on, and pulled it off.

It was the face of Tad, yet the normally bright green eyes glowed a malevolent red, and the face was pale and sickly, as though a great strain had been placed upon the body. Yet the shadows of the face were darker than normal, the shades of the eyes seemed more black than they ought to have, and the smile seemed dark and evil.

Bobert froze for a minute, uncertain, but the chaos of the Beast's escape had grown around him, and he needed to act fast. With one mighty blow, he brought the flat of his sword down on Tad's head, and his friend collapsed limply to the ground.

Looking around the clearing, Bobert saw that the Lizards were in disarray, as those who had been hit by the poison, which was a large portion of the ones at one end of the arena, flailed around in pain, and others tried not to step in the pools of acidic poison slowly spreading over the ground. This was made worse by the Beast's poison lighting any wood that it touched aflame, which meant that most of the forest around the clearing was now on fire, and that fire was spreading quickly by way of the fallen leaves. The smoke from this was clouding the forest, and making the chaos all the more tangible.

Furthermore, at the other end of the clearing, Bobert's Heroes had taken advantage of the Beast's escape to make their own, and had pulled out their concealed weapons to turn on their guards. Dante with a concealed knife had cut their rope bonds, and Bjorn had broken a few links on Sir Beren's shackles. Now they all fell in around Bobert, looking to him for leadership as the forest around them went up in flames and chaos. Bobert, of course, suggested they do the only thing they could do in a situation like that:

Run.

At least half an hour passed before Bobert stopped running, and stopped to take in the state of his group. They were all accounted for, thankfully, and all unharmed, even Tad, who was being carried like a doll by Bjorn. A few of them had obtained weapons, though they were not of a very high quality, and Grogory had obtained an axe with which he seemed to be surprisingly proficient. They were still all stript of armor, including Tad, whose crimson armor had been hurriedly removed by Dante and Sir Beren, so that Bjorn could run with him more easily.

After a brief check of each of his companions to ensure none were harmed, other than the angry welt on Tad's head, Bobert turned to the area they found themselves in. They had come to a gentle stream which flowed through the forest, trickling along blissfully ignorant of the evils which occurred around it. He did not recognize this part of the forest, and concluded that they must have been far, far from Croak and its familiar woods. But they were not out of danger yet. Search parties of Lizards were inevitable, and if they did not keep moving, they would undoubtedly be caught. He decided to follow the stream, since that would allow them to retrace their steps back towards the Lizards' camp if they had to.

They walked along the smooth, water-worn shore for what seemed like hours, until even Bjorn began to show signs of exhaustion;

he went from tucking Tad protectively under his arm to gently carrying Tad like a heavy load, to finally slinging his limp body over his shoulder like a bag of grain. Dante was lagging behind, and Sir Beren was stumbling now and then into Cat, who walked half-asleep behind him. At last, they came to a large, ivy-covered rockface from which the stream flowed, and when Bobert paused to look around, considering which way to go now that they couldn't follow the stream, Amphibia spoke.

"Bobert, we have to rest," she said quietly. "Grogory can barely stand, and I don't know how much longer the Giant can carry Tad."

Bobert glanced back at his exhausted men, and nodded.

"You're right, of course. But we can't stay out in the open like this. The Warlord will regain control of its men, and send out search parties soon. It'll want us and the Beast both. We need somewhere to sleep through the night where we won't be noticed."

"I wonder if there's a cave around here," Amphibia said, eyeing the rockface.

"The stream might have eroded large enough of a passage for us to stay there," Bobert answered. "It must be flowing from an underground lake or something. Keep an eye on Tad while I check it out."

Bobert waded into the chilly stream, gritting his teeth at the pain of the freezing water, and waded towards the cliff. To his surprise, though it looked small from the shore, the cavity from which the stream flowed was actually fairly large, so that even Bjorn could fit through it. He went in, wading deeper until the painfully cold water was up to his waist, but just when he thought the way might be too small, the tunnel widened. As his eyes adjusted to the dark, he saw that it was wide and shallow, and that there was a beach ahead in a turn in the stream, large enough for them to camp on comfortably.

He waded back out of the cave, and directed the rest how to get to the beach. As they entered the chilly stream single file, crying out at how cold the water was, Bobert went further into the tree line and collected dry wood, and found a sturdy branch which he quickly carved into a rough spear. Going back to the stream, his companions had all disappeared into the cliff-face, and the water had become once more undisturbed. Setting aside his dry wood to protect it from any splashes, Bobert used his rough spear and began to hunt fish. They were not very large in this stream, but they were lazy and bright, and it was not long before he had caught enough for them all to eat. As he cleaned the fish and found some sticks to stick them through, he stumbled across a bush ripe with fall berries, and some of the local root vegetables that he uprooted carefully.

He went back to the hidden beach, taking care to keep the wood dry so that it would not smoke very much, and built a large hole fire to warm their freezing limbs. While the flame grew, he finished cleaning the fish, rubbing them with the berries for flavor, and placing the root vegetables, which were cleaned in the stream, in slices upon the fish, so as to mingle their hopefully appetizing flavors. Bobert may have been a rough and tumble folk hero with a bad habit of emotional withdrawal and a drinking problem, but the man still liked a good meal, and he was a surprisingly good cook.

He sat back against the cave wall as the fish cooked over the fire, enjoying the wonderful sweet smell that slowly filled the cave, and falling into a light stupor as the warm, sweet air washed over his exhausted senses. He sleepily floated in and out of consciousness, and hardly seemed to notice when Amphibia settled beside him.

"Smells good," she said.

"It should be done soon," Bobert answered.

"Thank you," she told him, and when he merely nodded in answer, she continued. "Should we try to wake Tad?"

Bobert looked over to the yet-unconscious Frog, and thought about the horrible red of his possessed eyes. "Do you think it's safe?"

Amphibia shrugged. "I don't know what to think these days. Everything is so unnatural now. Magics and monsters, they make everything harder, more complicated."

"What good is life if it isn't hard?" Bobert asked. "Sure, you may be comfortable in an easy life, but will you ever really grow?"

Amphibia nodded, but it was Grogory who answered.

"Life is change. To change is to grow, and to grow is to live. But ease is stagnant, and therefore closer to death than life."

The three sat in brooding silence for a moment, until Grogory spoke again.

"I think Tad will probably be safe. If his connection was to the Beast, then it will fade as the Beast goes further away, and if he was made a puppet by the Warlord or one of its minions, then the distance from the camp should break the connection."

Bobert glanced between Amphibia and Grogory, and shrugged. Getting to his feet, he poked Dante and Cat awake, and went towards the cave mouth to tell Sir Beren, who was sitting watch, that they intended to awaken Tad. When all of them were gathered and awake, Amphibia mysteriously produced some smelling salts from about her person, and wafted them gently under Tad's nose.

Tad came around, blinking confusedly around as he took in the strange cave where he had woken up. He focused blearily on the faces of his fellows gazing concernedly, somewhat apprehensive down on him, and coughed painfully, gently feeling the wound on his head.

"What is this?" he asked. "Where are we?"

"You were captured by the Warlord," Bobert answered.

"I know that. I remember."

"Can you tell us what happened after you were captured?" Bobert asked.

Tad shook his head, looking confused.

"I don't know," he said. "I don't remember much. I was dragged before the Warlord in its hall of bone, ridiculed and beaten and spit on. I was questioned, but I would tell it nothing. So another was summoned, a black-robed creature with a chilly voice. It did… something to me. I can not remember. It was like fingers pushed into my head, into my senses. My sight was darkened; my touch was dulled. All I felt was anger, an ancient and primal anger. At times it burnt cooler, and at times it burnt so hot it seemed I could feel it, and I feared I would die. And when at last the veil lifted, I slept, until I woke here."

For a somber moment all were silent, until Grogory roused himself.

"You describe a possession in every key manner, Tad. Though why the spirit left you, I should like to know."

"Indeed, how can we be certain that the spirit has left at all?" Cat asked suspiciously.

BOBERT AND THE WARLORD

"Because unlike you," Amphibia replied sharply, "Spirits have minds. Everyone knows that the soul of a spirit is too large to squeeze into a Frog's body."

"Indeed," Grogory interjected gently. "A possession almost always carries physical signs; a sickly appearance, strangely colored eyes. It is almost always in the eyes, for their connection to the soul. Now, a lesser spirit can share a creature's body without such signs, but any spirit strong enough to take a body by force is too strong to hide therein."

"So I am free of this spirit?" Tad asked.

"I do not know," Grogory replied, looking worried. "You are not possessed now, this much is certain. But I fear there may be scars on your mind that will only heal with time."

"My mind is fine," Tad growled. "I will see this battle through. I want to find this Warlord. I want to kill it."

After a brief meal and a long rest, Bobert and his Heroes, plus honorary members Amphibia and Grogory, debated their next move. Sir Beren and Cat proposed a rush of the camp, an all-out assault until they beat through the Lizards and slew their leader. Dante and Tad, naturally, were reluctant to enter into a battle they could not hope to win, and proposed instead returning to Croak, and from their seeking allies to join their war. Amphibia knew a frontal assault would only lead to their deaths, but found the wait to gather an army impractical; by the time an army was gathered, Croak would have burnt. Grogory thought the wisest course of action was to consult a book.

Bobert listened to them argue silently, considering each point for himself, but his favored plan of action came not from them, but from Bjorn.

"What if the camp has changed?" the Giant rumbled worriedly. "What if there are more nasty Lizards now, or if they are still in chaos? Shouldn't we see what they are doing, before we decide what to do ourselves?"

"A wise assertion, amico," Dante agreed. "We must know the army that we seek to defeat. We need to know their strengths and weaknesses."

"How much could change in a few hours?" Cat protested. "We must strike now before we lose the element of surprise, and the advantage of their chaos!"

"And should their chaos and our surprise not be enough?" Tad asked grimly. "Should sheer numbers overwhelm us and all be taken, should we be subjected one and all to the fate I have only just escaped? What hope has Croak then? Who rescues the rescuers?"

"There remain good men in that camp!" Sir Beren cried. "Monks who took me in and nurtured me, and now sit caged like criminals! We cannot just let them rot there!"

"Our deaths will do them no good," Bobert interjected into the conversation, causing all to fall silent. "Bjorn is right; we need a clearer picture of the situation, before we make a plan."

"And how are we to get that?" Cat asked. "Shall we sneak into the camp, and scout it out in disguise? Or perhaps bribe a menial soldier within the camp to tell us all he knows?"

"Or we return to where we began," Bobert answered impatiently. "The clearing from which the whole camp may be seen. Even if they have found it, I doubt any watch will be kept on it. They believe we have long since fled for Croak."

So, their bodies rested and their bellies filled, Bobert's Heroes hid all traces of their camp in the hidden cave[20], and began the long journey back towards the Lizard's camp.

Bobert et all got back to the clearing long after night had fallen, and found that the clearing appeared to have been swiftly searched while they were gone, but Bobert and Sir Beren had done a good enough job of covering up their tracks, and Cat a good enough job of hiding their armor, that the Lizards had quickly moved on, and their equipment had

---

[20] It is a well-established fact that hidden caves are discovered at least monthly, and some studies have suggested that 90% of all hidden caves contain two or more buried treasures. Similar studies have suggested that up to 33% of the world's wealth is buried in hidden caves. And yet other studies have suggested that up to 75% of all study citations are in fact based upon no real study.

remained undiscovered and undisturbed. As they all settled down to rest, Bobert snuck over to the edge of the clearing and peered down into the camp.

Though many of the Lizards had returned to their normal duties in the camp, an overwhelming portion of them appeared to still be out, and in the dark of the forest Bobert could see dozens of little lights, spread out beneath the trees in a jagged, curved line, which he knew were the search parties that were trying to find him and his men. He had run into difficulty avoiding those parties, and had been forced to lead his men far out of the way to go around them, and to hope that by the time it was light enough for the night-blind Lizards to see the prints, they would be well away.

The defenses of the camp were as strong as ever, and it seemed that they had been beefed up a little, which would make it even more difficult for Bobert to sneak in, and search for the book and prisoners from the monastery, which he knew were the most important things to focus on right now.

His companions were all asleep by now, but Bobert did not rest. Instead, as he contemplated sleeplessly how to best get back into the camp with no more than the eight of them, his eye was caught by movement below, in the woods near the camp. Fearing that it was a patrol, and that he had best keep an eye on it, lest it manage to sneak up and catch them while they were all sleeping, he watched the area intently, alert for any other sign of movement. He saw it again, quick and stealthy, and knew that this was no Lizard. He went over and woke Sir Beren, telling him to keep watch, and then snuck out of the clearing, down to where he saw the movement.

He stopped behind a tree a few feet away, and saw a group of stealthy figures in black, whispering together and eyeing the Lizard's camp. The figures seemed to be debating the camp's defenses, and appeared to be some kind of a scouting party. Bobert snuck around them, hoping to get a look at their faces, but as he moved, one of them, who appeared to be their leader, stood suddenly and drew a sword.

"Reveal yourself, now, or I'll run you through and reveal you myself."

Bobert smiled widely at hearing the Frog's voice, for he recognized it immediately as Gramps, a senior ranger at the Council of Forest Rangers. The Council, and the rangers who served it, operated under the directive to protect and serve the Frogs of King Gulk's kingdom, and the forests on which Gulk's people relied. Whether in a battle against invading mice or forest fires, the rangers sought constantly to protect and serve the people. When Bobert was yet young, he had sought some training from the Council, and Gramps had taken him on. He had taught Bobert a great deal in the ways of being a hero, and had played an instrumental role in making Bobert the Frog he was today, and though Bobert had turned his back on the Council, and worked with them only occasionally, still he and Gramps were as close as ever.

"Now is that any way to greet your old friend, Gramps?" Bobert asked innocently. "I see the years haven't improved your hospitality."

The other rangers watched Bobert suspiciously, and their hands strayed to their weapons, but Gramps lowered his sword and chuckled.

"Shoulda known you'd be wrapped up in this. Ain't nothing that goes down in Croak without you knowing, is there?"

"I wouldn't be a very good hero if there was, now would I? Question is, how did *you* know about this?"

"The Council got a letter saying that a large force of Lizards had appeared, and they sent me to investigate, with a small army of rangers. We got here a few hours ago, but something had just gone down. I saw something winging its way towards the mountains, and search parties of Lizards came through, several of them, all scouring the area. Took all of our skill not to get caught. Anyway, the search parties moved off, but their defenses seem to be impenetrable from here."

"Ah, that might have been us. I may have freed their war beast accidentally, while in the process of escaping. But this isn't the place for a story. Come back to my camp, and we can speak. You can get a better view of the camp's defenses from there too."

Gramps acquiesced, and they made their way back to the clearing. All of Bobert's men were up when they got back, and Sir Beren appeared to have woken them, for none of them were speaking to him. Sir Beren at some point had built a hole fire as well, covered with a large cloak to minimize the light, and he had made coffee, which Bobert accepted gratefully.

BOBERT AND THE WARLORD

"Gramps?" Amphibia asked in surprise, when he entered the clearing behind Bobert. "When did you get here? What are you doing here?"

Gramps chuckled, and greeted Amphibia as an old friend, and then introduced himself to the rest of the group.

"Name's Gilbert, but these two call me Gramps." He jerked his thumb at Bobert, "This one started it, thought it was funny, and as he introduced Amphibia and me, she picked it up. These fellers," he jerked his thumb at the other rangers, "call me sir. You can call me what you want. I don't care about you enough to care either way."

He turned to Bobert, "Who are these anyway? Last I heard you never ran with a crew."

Bobert shook his head sadly. "Never needed one before now, but lately stuff has been getting so bad I had to form one. Meet Bjorn Giant, he's the giant, as you can probably guess, and Dante, who are constant companions. This is Sir Beren, he's a monk who is fighting a holy war or something silly like that. Tad just got bored in retirement. Cat Frills, of course, is a Forest Ranger, you probably know him. You know Amphibia, of course, and this is Grogory, who is actually Croak's librarian, but felt that he should accompany us to ensure that certain things were handled properly."

Gramps glanced at Cat strangely, and Cat smiled back awkwardly. The others made their greetings, until Grogory, who said, "I'm glad to know I still have some pull at the Council of Rangers. Many of my peers have been denounced as fools by your Council, but I suppose I've kept my head down well enough. I didn't expect such a snappy reply to my letter, but I won't complain."

Gramps sized Grogory up.

"So you're the one who asked the Council for help, eh? That's good. I have a fairly good idea of the situation, I think, but I won't mind hearing your full story."

"If you want the full story, you'll have to sit through three, none from me. Bobert's first, and you'll see, I hope, why I sent the letter. He had come to me, along with Cat and Amphibia, and had told me many odd things. I asked to come with them, so as to see first hand what happened, but before we left my library I sent off my letter, thinking it likely that help would be appreciated, and prudent to seek it then, if what I suspected was accurate, namely that the larger force of

Lizards was much larger than Bobert seemed to think. He feared a tribe. I feared an army. And it looks like I was right. But I have explained myself, now Bobert may tell his tale, and Dante his, and finally Tad, in order from most to least informative, that you may not be kept in suspense too long."

So Gramps was caught up on all the many events which had occurred since the monk had sought Bobert's help. Due to a regular correspondence with both Bobert and Amphibia, Gramps already knew of the rising levels of aggressive creatures in Croak, but even he was surprised to hear of a massacre at a monastery, and when Bobert got to the sorcerer, Gramps eyes darkened as memories of old battles and old losses came back to him. When the stories were over, Gramps immediately had a course of action.

"Well, well. I don't like the sound of this. You eight have been busy doing my job. Not that I'm complaining. You've done a fine job, and made my next move easy to determine. Right now, everything bad is in that camp, save the Beast. But that strange creature is no doubt far from here by now. We will hunt it later. For now this camp should be the priority."

"The Beast was only beaten and abused in the camp," Bobert agreed. "It isn't coming back."

"So here's what I say we do," Gramps continued. "And I don't mean to step on any toes, Bobert. As far as I'm concerned this is your operation; we're just the backup. But this is my idea. I say we go into this camp in full force, and in one fateful attack we take out this Warlord, this Sorcerer, and as many Lizards as we can. We release the prisoners, and we secure the Book. I don't know what it is, but in my experience, if a sorcerer wants it, I don't want them to have it."

Bobert nodded. "That all sounds well and good, but how do you suppose we get into the camp? You've seen the defenses. Need another look? We got a great view from here."

Bobert expected a retort from Gramps, but it was Tad who spoke.

"I remember one time, in my days in the King's army, when we received orders to take a city. Now, this city had big stone walls and plenty of people to hold them, and we weren't a big force, so we couldn't waste too many men trying to scale the walls like ants. The sewers, our next go-to, were already blocked, they seemed to have thought of that. Not to mention that they were already on the lookout for us, so sneaking in wasn't gonna work. One of our leaders suggested we build a giant wooden fish, but everyone else said that was dumb. Finally, they managed to get a single scout in, and he reported that there was an oil store right next to one of the gates. So we sent him back in, and told him to light one of the barrels. We hoped that a raging fire through the city would weaken their defenses. He lit the barrels, and the force of the explosion blew a hole right through that wall."

Bobert thought for a moment, and smiled.

"You know what Tad, I think that just might work. All right Gramps, let's do this."

Midnight came, and with it a signal, a flaming arrow shot high into the air, which fell into the middle of the camp. Four other flaming arrows swiftly followed the first, though they fell not into the camp. They were aimed, instead, at the tops of each gates, where they struck, thanks to the expert marksmanship of the bowmen who shot them, the sealed barrels of oil that were stored there to defend against besiegers.

When a combustible material begins to burn, it undergoes an exothermic reaction, that is, it releases more energy than was required to initiate the burning. When such a reaction takes place in a closed container, the result is a violent expansion of the material to the limits of the container, and a huge buildup of pressure as the reaction continues without room to expand.

The violence of such a reaction is based largely off of the material burning and the material constricting. In this case, oil does not release huge amounts of energy, and wooden barrels are not particularly sturdy. However, a third factor must also be accounted for, which is the amount of material present. In this case, it was huge stockpiles of oil barrels. So while the result was not as violent a reaction as may have occurred with other materials, it was enough to create a sonic disturbance that chattered the teeth of every creature within a mile.

More accurately, they went **BOOM**.

All four gates were blown out and the bridges were all destroyed, effectively cutting off every way into and out of the camp.

Burning shrapnel was also flung throughout the camp, lighting the tent city ablaze with swiftly spreading fire.

The camp descended into chaos as fires erupted all over the place, and spread quickly thanks to the cloth and fur of the tents. Lizards began to rush about, some trying to put out the fires, some trying to escape them, some taking advantage of the chaos to steal from the others, as is the nature of Lizards. Those trying to escape soon realised that the bridges had been destroyed, and this added to the panic. A smoky haze rose over the camp, and the fire spread further through the tents, and lit the wooden walls outside of which a large group of rangers moved forward, and dropped a pre-built bridge across the trench, allowing them to cross over. Several took up guard positions on either side of the temporary bridge, and the rest pushed forward, drawing their weapons to slay any Lizards they saw.

Bobert's Heroes crossed the bridge next, and spread out in groups, a random ranger attaching himself to Cat. They pushed through the camp quickly, slaying any Lizards in their way or who tried to stop them in their search for the Lizards' prisoners. Bobert's Heroes saved many prisoners from the flames that day, escorting them back to the bridge and seeing them over safely, and then diving back in to find more. The Lizards, not being an actual army, but a group of tribes and families united under the Warlord's banner by his strength alone, did not have a single prisoner wagon. Instead, each tribe, family, or minor warlord had their own prisoners which they had captured during raids, and presumably which they intended to use as slaves after their long raiding expedition.

Sir Beren and Tad had the particular honor of freeing the prisoners that the Lizards had taken from the monastery, but, despite Tad's protests, the Praying Mantes would not consent to be taken back to the bridge and safety. Instead, they had Sir Beren remove their chains, and they shirked their heavy over-robes, revealing lighter, less restricting robes beneath. They moved off, promising to join the fight and make the Lizards pay for violating their monastery with unholy acts. Tad thought this terribly foolish, until he saw one Lizard passing by get caught, in the blink of an eye, by the claws of a Praying Mantis, and get ripped limb from limb as the monk settled into a pleasant, if somewhat hurried, snack.

The last over the bridge were Bobert and Amphibia, accompanied by Gramps and, to everyone's surprise, Grogory. These four focused neither on the Lizards, who were already being routed quite effectively by the Rangers, nor on the prisoners, who were being rescued swiftly by Bobert's Heroes. No, Bobert and his companions focused instead on reaching the center of the camp, and the center of the problem.

In the courtyard before the entrance to its grand bone hall, the Warlord was shouting orders. It was trying to corral the Lizards in the courtyard, trying to command them to form bucket chains to quench the fires, using water from the wells they had dug throughout the camp, or to go to the walls and attempt to repair the damage while the enemy was preoccupied with the escaped prisoners. It was also trying to form a brute squad, which would accompany it personally while it hunted down the Rangers and Praying Mantes one by one. Unfortunately, the majority of the Lizards were too undisciplined to listen to its commands, and it was having a difficult time controlling even those nearest it. It was surrounded by chaos, and it wasn't at all hard for Bobert and his companions to approach not only unseen, but unnoticed.

"You know, this is why Frogs actually *train* our soldiers. It works way better."

The Warlord whipped around, and saw Bobert standing on the other side of the courtyard, with Amphibia, Gramps, and Grogory flanking him. Pure anger flashed in the Warlord's eyes, and it emitted such a powerful roar of rage that many of the Lizards in the clearing turned to see the disturbance. Spotting the Frogs, the Lizards began to draw their weapons and approach, vengeance in their eyes.

The Warlord laughed an angry and triumphant laugh. "So you're the one behind this. I should've known. Well, you're here now. Come here, so I can rip you limb from filthy limb!"

The Warlord rushed forward and made a grab at Bobert, but with the lightness of one who often fights with beings much larger than him, Bobert skipped to the side, and drew his sword. The Warlord spun, and drew the largest mace Bobert had ever seen, the head of which was easily as large as his body. In its other hand it wielded the enormous shield which had hung in its hall, and the red diamond in the dragon's mouth swam with the light of the fires, almost hypnotically distracting Bobert as the Warlord donned a heavy helmet, which was shaped to look like the Beast's head, and then swung its mace around to hit Bobert.

The hero dodged as the Warlord struck, and turned to see the mace buried in the ground where he had just been. With a great yank the Warlord pulled the mace from the ground, leaving an odd crater with sharp ridges within it, which Bobert knew represented his own destiny if he was even nicked by that terrible weapon. Bobert and the Warlord began their dance, looking oddly like a bad game of whack-a-mole.

While Bobert was occupied with the Warlord, Amphibia and Grogory engaged the many Lizards which were approaching. Amphibia, her bow broken in a previous escapade[21] with Bobert, now fought with two long knives, one a gift from Bobert and one stolen from him. Beside her, Grogory fought with the axe that he had stolen from a Lizard when they had escaped their chains earlier. Amphibia danced with grace through the Lizards, slicing them so quickly that they didn't realize they were harmed until blood swelled from their chests. Grogory, on the other hand, was far more frightful for his lack of grace, as he rushed through the Lizards swinging his axe like a madman, a bloodlust on him like none Amphibia had ever seen. The Lizards attempted to retreat from this awkward and angry little Frog, but had fire behind them where their tents were burning. So instead, they fell to Grogory's complete lack of finesse and technique, most with missing limbs or broken skulls. Every blow that Grogory swung was punctuated with his mumblings, most of which took the form 'You think you can mess with my books?... I'll burn *you*, how'd *you* like it?... Books are the lifeblood of culture, I can tell you've been without them for altogether too long, you uncouth barbarians.'

Such a great number of Lizards fell to Grogory's rampage and Amphibia's finesse that Gramps, who was observing the scene, did not see any point in joining their slaughter. He was turning to instead search the Warlord's hall while everyone was distracted, but a flash of

---

[21] Bobert and the Silversmith. You really ought to read it. You know, since this is the sequel...

movement at the other side of the courtyard caught his eye instead, and he saw a wisp of black cloak as it whipped out of sight, passing among the burning tents. Gramps, remembering Bobert's tale from earlier, thought to himself that he must have seen the Sorcerer, and he went to give pursuit. Gritting his teeth, he leapt through the flames, and came to a small clearing in the tents, in which the Sorcerer crouched, reading a book aloud, which Gramps quickly realised was The Book, and which was on the ground before him.

Gramps watched, frozen in place as the Sorcerer began to read from the Book, enunciating each word as though it were the highest honor, reading as though from a holy text. Each word was backed with passion, each sound formed from pure emotion, as though all the Sorcerer's soul was poured into the power of the Book.

The fire from the tents in the clearing began to wash towards the Sorcerer like fallen leaves in the fall, swirling around him as though caught in a whipping wind. The fire became a swirling, flashing whirlwind, and something began to grow within, a darkness that was completely unnatural, like pure shadow within the flame. The darkness became solid as if it took on flesh, coalescing into a being within the sorcerous firestorm, a being of shadow with menacing red eyes.

The terror of this creature woke Gramps from his stupor, and he leapt forward with his sword held aloft, shouting a war cry to startle his foe. The Sorcerer whipped around, dropping the Book he had held so reverently, and immediately the fire collapsed and extinguished, and the dark figure within was gone. Gramps struck down hard with his sword, and the Sorcerer threw his hands up in a protective gesture. Magic, however, held no charm over cold steel, and Gramps' sword cleaved into his foe, leaving him dead.

Gramps surveyed the area, but the Lizards had still not noticed him, and he was alone. Kneeling, he cut the hood from the Sorcerer's robes, and wrapped the Book in it, tucking the bundle into his armor, before he turned and returned carefully to the courtyard and the battle raging there.

In the brief time it had taken Gramps to slay the Sorcerer, Amphibia and Grogory had slain the majority of the Lizards, and were in the midst of fighting the small groups that were still brave enough to gang up on them. Bobert, meanwhile, was fighting the Warlord, though he certainly seemed to have gained the upper hand. The Warlord now had cuts on both of its arms and on the back of one leg, which it knelt on to avoid putting weight on. Bobert was skipping around the Warlord, but could not get close enough again to strike, for every time he tried the Warlord swung its mace and cut Bobert off. As he circled, trying to find an opening past the shield, Bobert spotted Gramps, and a silent agreement passed between them. Bobert jumped forward, and the Warlord began to swing its mace. Gramps took a running start, and jumped forward, stabbing his sword straight into the Warlord's back, through its spine between its shoulder blades, and into its heart. The Warlord froze, and looked down at its chest, then grasped Gramps' blade with two fingers, and broke the tip off where it stuck out of its chest. The Warlord grinned a terrible grin, and flicked the blade shard away. Bobert backed away, uncertain. That blow, after all, should most certainly have killed even the Warlord. Nothing, not even a Lizard, could survive a blow through the spine and into the heart.

As the Warlord got back to its feet, all of its wounds seemed to heal, and it hefted its shield without any sign of weakness. The rubies of the dragon shield's eyes no longer glowed, for the fires in the camp had begun to die, but the brilliant red diamond in the mouth of the shield yet glowed, as if with a life of its own. In fact, it seemed as though the light within was boiling, straining against its crystalline confines. It seemed strange to Bobert, for there was now no light for the diamond to reflect, yet it seemed to glow only brighter.

As if the thought were placed in Bobert's very head, a memory rose unbidden into his mind, the memory of the gem that the Necromancer had used in channeling his magic. Perhaps, he thought, this diamond served some similar purpose. Perhaps it was what gave the Warlord such terrible strength. So when next the Warlord swung his mace, Bobert leapt forwards. The giant Lizard caught the hero on his shield, but Bobert had planned on it. He grasped the shield's edge with his hands, lodged one boot into the dragon's mouth, and with the steel toe of the other, he kicked the diamond as hard as he could.

His suspicions of the gem's magical nature were confirmed when the diamond shattered, and the force threw him off the shield, twisting his leg at the knee. The Warlord stumbled back, and with a look of pure rage glanced between Bobert and the diamond.

BOBERT AND THE WARLORD

A great wind went up, at that moment, carrying the flame around them to relight other tents. The wind screamed through the branches of the trees in the forest like a thousand freed prisoners. The wind passed as a second began. This second wind caught up the pieces of diamond, whipping them to and fro in a wide cycle as they began to dissolve. As the second wind died, the last piece of diamond dissolved, and the Warlord seemed to shrink, to grow weak and defeated. A third wind came after that. It swirled around the Warlord like he was caught in a cyclone, and began to pull from him a shadow, which screamed its protest, and twisted and fought, then disappeared with a flash into the ruins of the camp, and the Warlord lay dead with its passing.

The next night, the Man in the Moon[22] rose to find nine exhausted warriors, resting in Amphibia's inn as they drank murky water and ate little candied ants. For a while they were too exhausted to speak, but eventually Amphibia's wonderful brew revitalized them, and they began to speak.

Sir Beren spoke first, addressing Bobert.

"I have thought much on what you said, Bobert, when we were marching to the Lizards' camp. I have done much good work with you, but my time is done. I am called back to the monastery, back to a life of peace and worship. I am thankful, both to you and to The Light One, that I could help you in this time, but my mission is over, the great menace is defeated, and my brothers need me."

The silence that followed Sir Beren's announcement was palpable, until Dante spoke. "Master Beren, I for one am greatly honored and pleased to have ever known and fought beside you. You are a man of true honor and wisdom, and I have learned much from your example, as I'm sure we all have."

---

[22] Much speculation surrounds the Man in the Moon. Why does he most often come out at night? Why does he sometimes come out during the day? Why does he float in the sky? Some have suggested that the Man in the Moon is not an actual person, but merely a very large rock. He takes great offense at this. In all honesty, the Man in the Moon is an incorrigible drunk, who mostly comes out at night because he drinks so much that he is passed out during the day, and he lives in the sky because he can't afford real estate, mostly due to his being an unemployed drunkard.

Dante looked around expectantly, but no one else seemed prepared to say anything, so he raised his glass in toast. "To Sir Beren! May you find peace in your monastery once more."

The others likewise toasted him, and Tad in an unexpected display of affection smiled at him. Sir Beren thanked them for their toast, and, eager to change the subject from him, turned to Tad. "And what shall you do, Tad? Now that Croak is out of danger, shall you continue with Bobert, merely for the adventure?"

Tad laughed and drained his cup. He was sitting at one of the tables with Gramps, and the two, to no one's surprise, were getting on incredibly well, mostly because Tad was the only person that Gramps had ever met older than him and still in fighting condition. "No, Sir Beren, I don't think I will. I may be able to fight still, but I don't want to. I'm done with that life, I had my fill in younger years. No, I'll leave the treasure and treachery up to Bobert here."

"You sure you won't stick around? Bobert could use someone with a good head to watch his back, you know," Gramps said. "Not to mention I wouldn't mind working with you more. It's hard finding good help."

Tad rose, and donned his cloak. "I appreciate the offer, Gramps, but I'm too old for this life. Next time there's an army on the doorstep, drop by. I'll be happy to help. For now, however, I think I'll go back to fancy drinks and long vacations. I heard that Polliwog Way is nice this time of year. Now, if you'll kindly excuse me, I'm off. I think I'll go home and have a nice relaxing bath. Don't laugh, Dante, real men take baths. It's only boys like you that don't think they're manly."

Bobert looked into his glass. He knew that he'd just lost two excellent fighters, but he hoped that he wouldn't need them again anyway. Still, he was sad to see them go. They had been through a lot together in the span of a few days, and he had developed a sort of brotherhood with them.

The silence was broken a few minutes later by Grogory, as he clambered tipsily off his barstool and towards the coat rack.

"Well, gentlemen, I think that I too shall retire from my brief yet brilliant stint as a hero. It turns out the adventurer's life is simply not for me. Besides, it seems to come with a bit too much drinking, and I seem to be tipsy after only two. My head feels oddly fuzzy, and I believe, but can not confirm, that I am swaying on the spot. I shall, however, wish to write this down. The adventure. Not the copious drinking. I'll want to talk to each of you in time. Get your stories in detail, and such. And the Book, this strange text, I intend to keep in the safety of my library. Well, if none have anything more to say to me, I shall take my leave."

As Grogory stepped out into the night, Cat too rose, apparently intending to leave, but he had not even begun his farewells when Gramps spoke.

"Not so fast, boy. There's a mystery here I'd rather like to solve. Namely that you claim to be a ranger, and I never taught you. Care to explain how that is? Cause you ain't old enough to have had ol' Merryweather who came before me."

Cat looked around shame-faced, like a child caught in a lie. Bobert could tell that he was nervous, right on the edge of breaking, and needed only a push. He set his cup down firmly, and Cat folded.

"Alright, so I'm no Ranger," Cat cried pleadingly to Bobert. "I just told you that so you'd let me join. I figured you would want someone with qualifications, and I didn't have any, but I knew I could help, if I was just given the chance, so I lied about being a fresh graduate, thinking that that would make it less suspicious if I didn't know stuff. By the time that Dante joined, and I realised you would have taken me without qualifications, I was already in so deep I figured I'd just ride it out and leave town when the whole thing was over."

Bobert smiled.

"I had already guessed, I hope you realize. I wanted to know how long you'd keep up the charade. Towards the end I wasn't sure if you were really dumb enough to think you could keep a secret from me, or if I was actually wrong about you. I told you your pride would be your downfall."

Cat gaped like a fish out of water, as did the rest of the group barring Gramps, all of whom were watching like they had bought tickets to a bad drama.

"How? How did you know? And how long?"

Bobert laughed at Cat's confusion.

"Well, you may think you're a good liar, but you aren't, Cat. There were too many inconsistencies, to be honest. How you can't wake yourself up at dawn, how you didn't know to dig a hole fire, how you lose all sense of direction after a short hike through the woods. Your inefficiency with close-range weaponry. No one could have gotten through training like that; you would have either flunked out or learned the skills. That, and how you claim to be a fresh graduate? Graduates aren't assigned their own area until their third year on the job, like you claimed you were, and I would have been asked if they wanted you to be my apprentice, even if the Council and eye don't always see eye to eye."

Gramps chuckled in his corner as he watched the others try to work out how they had never noticed that Cat was lying. Cat, however, was confused for an entirely different reason.

"Why did you let me join then? Or stay in? Why didn't you say anything?"

Bobert took a thoughtful draw from his tankard before he answered.

"Well, you showed me what you could do with that bow. That was part of it. Plus, you were so intent on helping that you lied. I doubted then and now whether refusing to let you join would have dissuaded you from helping. Letting you join was the only way I could keep an eye on you and make sure you didn't get yourself killed."

Cat nodded thoughtfully.

"I probably would have followed you around and joined the fight whenever one broke out anyway."

Bobert laughed.

"I know. It's what I did, at your age. Question is, what do we do with you now? After all, you lied to me, nearly got me killed, and have only a handful of actually useful skills."

Bobert hummed to himself thoughtfully as Cat wilted, looking simultaneously ashamed, disappointed, and resigned.

"Very well, Bobert. You needn't drag this out. I shall leave. Cat Frills may be a fool, but I'll retain what little honor I have left, if it's all the same to you."

Cat turned to leave. Gramps harrumphed and Dante coughed quietly. Amphibia looked pleased, for she had developed an intense dislike for Cat since Bobert's adventure with a certain vine-zipline. Bobert, however, merely laughed once more, as Cat walked away.

BOBERT AND THE WARLORD

"If you want to retain your honor, Cat, you don't do it by walking away. I never said I didn't want you. Actually, I quite like you. I'm just not sure whether you'd do better becoming an *actual* Ranger or simply staying with me. Well, best of both worlds. You're going with Gramps, if you'll consent. He'll teach you just like he taught me, all the ways of the Rangers, on the job. I've no doubt he'll mind, he always likes fresh meat. You'll learn how to actually do this job, and you'll get to help people like you wanted. Gramps, do you like the sound of this?"

Gramps confirmed his assent, and all eyes were turned to Cat. He thought for a moment, before answering.

"Okay. Okay, I'll do it. I'll follow Gramps and learn everything he has to teach, until Cat Frills is the greatest Ranger to have ever lived!"

Gramps and Bobert exchanged a tired look, as Amphibia rolled her eyes. Gramps got to his feet.

"Alright, calm down boy. I want to sleep first. Bobert, it was good seeing you, kid. You too, Amphibia. I'll be writing the Council tomorrow, telling them I'm sticking around for a while. I want to know what that Book is about. I want to hunt this Beast down as well, not to mention figuring out just what it is that's drawing so many phenomena to Croak, of all places."

With that Gramps left, and Cat strolled out behind him. Another half hour passed in pleasant conversation, before Dante rose, and Bjorn with him.

"I apologize that we have no big speech planned, amici. We were planning on staying, for lack of anything better to do. I believe that more will go down before this is over. Sì, we shall be, how do you say, hanging around, for the end. The grand finale, I believe it is called, when the corpulent madame shall sing?"

Bobert and Amphibia, the only ones left besides them, thanked them both for their help, and assured them that they would be glad to have it in the future. The inn door closed behind them, and Bobert turned to Amphibia, who sat beside him at the bar, sipping a goblet of her finest muck.

"How long do you think it is before they all realise that you're the only lodging in town?"

Amphibia laughed.

"It won't be too long. There's not many other places to check."

Bobert laughed with her, and the two settled into a comfortable silence for a few minutes more.

"You did a good thing today, Bobert. That warlord was a menace. The world will be better without it."

"That's not what I'm thinking about, actually. Did you happen to see it die?"

"No, I was a bit preoccupied, what with a Lizard trying to murder me and all."

"An understandable reason to miss anything, I would say. Do you recall the shield that hung above it throne?"

Amphibia nodded.

"Well, it was carrying that in the courtyard, do you remember? When I was battling it, Gramps came back, and while I distracted the Warlord, Gramps leapt upon its back, and stabbed it through where its heart at least should have been."

"Go on," Amphibia prompted.

"It didn't die."

Amphibia choked on her drink.

"What do you mean it didn't die?"

"I mean it reached up and broke the tip off of Gramps' sword where it stuck through its chest, and then it kept fighting like it was nothing. And then, I don't know why, but I thought about the Necromancer, and how he only died when I broke his emerald. And then my eyes fell on the red diamond in the mouth of the shield. So, almost instinctively, I jumped on the shield, and kicked the diamond. When the diamond shattered, the Warlord collapsed and died, as though the only thing keeping it alive had been taken away. And the diamond, just like the Necromancer's emerald, dissolved in the wind. Now, I don't like reading into this stuff, but that weird sort of stuff doesn't happen in exactly the same way in the same year in the same place without being connected."

"So what? You think they had the same, I don't know, patron?"

"If I had to guess? I'd say the Necromancer struck a deal. The Warlord, on the other hand, well, a lot of the Lizard religions worship stuff we'd call demons. Maybe the Warlord worshipped the same being

BOBERT AND THE WARLORD

the Necromancer made a deal with. The question is, what does this mystery demon, this Shade, want with Croak?"

The End

Epilogue

The Shade flicked through trees, and came upon a scene of carnage. Normally, a scene such as this would please It greatly, or at least mildly amuse It, but this particular scene represented the defeat of Its latest general, and the Shade did not like defeat. Defeat was for the weak, the meek, the humble. It was none of these things. Defeat, in essence, was unacceptable.

It was that pesky hero again, It knew. It could taste his presence. He had had help this time, for the one that had killed Its sorcerer during the summoning had not been the same one that had destroyed Death. No, the hero appeared to have built a team to battle Its generals. A successful team. Now, the Shade knew, It would have to throw Its full force against the hero. It apparently could not count on Its warriors to hunt him down and slay him, nor on Its sorcerers to destroy him with magic. Even Its generals seemed to fall like dominoes before the staggering gait of the drunken sot of a hero. So be it. If It could not destroy his body, it would do just as well to destroy his mind. That would, after all, be quite satisfying.

The Shade wondered how best to go about breaking the hero's mind as It wove Its way out of the still smoldering wreckage of War's camp. It slipped out of the camp and came to the Altar. Now two arches

BOBERT AND THE WARLORD

were collapsed, the northern one and the southern one. It wondered which of Its last two generals to summon first.

It slipped away from the Ruins, and came to the little Frog village, and suddenly, like a fire sparks in the depths of the woods, like a tentacle stirs in the darkest waters, like a daemon pulls itself out of the confines of the darkest prison, an idea formed.

Yes, that would do. This hero could handle one at a time, and perhaps two. Feats of strength were not his shortcoming. No, no, his shortcoming was something else, was the greatest weakness of all of the sapient species; a complete ignorance of the right of power and might, a foolish belief in make-believe morality, a constant struggle with good and evil. So It made Its plan. Two generals, one terrible choice. Their lives, or the lives of all his people.

The Shade lurked in the street and watched a mother pampering her little daughters, and thought to Itself that they would do nicely.

As Dante would say, Finite.

www.ingramcontent.com/pod-product-compliance
Lightning Source LLC
Chambersburg PA
CBHW071942120726
48001CB00005B/2008